SETTLEMEN

MARTIN NA

SPUYTEN DUYVIL
New York City

ary of Congress Cataloging-in-Publication Data

ll, Martin.
ement / Martin Nakell.
n.
 978-1-933132-10-5
cial interaction--Fiction. 2. City planning--Fiction.
perimental fiction. I. Title.

64.A5314S48 2007
54--dc22

007328

Settlement

So. I arrived here during the time of the Emergency Orders, assigned to head up the same Bureau I had once worked in before the Emergency, now overseeing the whole Settlement. On that first day, after settling the issue of proper papers, identification, assignment of offices, and so on, I wandered the streets to get a feel for the mood in the Settlement. Remember? Sitting within the stone rubble of a collapsed building—collapsed by violence or simply disuse?—a young couple, holding two paper cups of coffee, were talking. The girl was laughing. Although I heard their words, they spoke a language I didn't understand. From what outpost might they have arrived? I walked past them—they didn't take notice of me—then I turned to pass them again. They spoke a fundamentally foreign language, not even of the same sounds or word-roots as my own. The girl, laughing loudly, teased and played with her young companion. When I got back to the Bureau I made notes in my personal notebook describing this first detail of life in the Emergency Settlement. I can look back at those notes now, thumbing through their pages as though they were alive, part of life, days, or weeks, or hours.

In a strange way I was glad to be here. I come from a small town. While I always liked living in the City, a part of me longed for something at once more open and at the same time more containable. Ironic: what I got for openness was an Emergency Settlement that I was now responsible to contain. Even more irony, because my desire for a small place arose largely out of a wish to live in a more intimate environment with my wife and daughter, not to share them so much with that large, distracting urban world. How is it I could have gone on working for the very Government that had taken my wife and daughter from me? That kept them from me? How could I? Was it because I couldn't throw hope away, even if it were a stupid, transparently vain hope? When they assigned me here, when they took my wife and daughter off with the others, I should have refused, I should have gone on the lam, I should have ditched everything.

No. It's certainly not hope that I'll be back together with my wife and daughter. It's hope that the Emergency will be declared over, that we'll go back to living. Even though I now know that the Emergency is perpetual. Why keep despair in check? It's an automatic response. Writing, even though I can't imagine to whom I'm writing, can't fathom that anyone will ever read this, still, writing is another way of coping with the despair. I almost said that writing was a way of stemming or defeating the despair. One would like to say that. Perhaps it's true. Maybe because I know that no one will ever read this I can be as honest as any man can allow himself to be. As honest as one person's own psychic equilibrium will allow.

I look back over what I just wrote. That no one will read this. Everything soon will be in ruin. This writing too, in ruin. A ruins. Are we drawn toward ruin? I have seen so much of ruin now in the last months that it seems like a natural condition, or one we ordain. But, as I write that I'm haunted by the girl I saw laughing with her boyfriend when I first came. And I'm haunted, of course, by Alina. Alina's absence. Is that why I'm writing, to make up for Alina's absence? To forgive myself? So many languages congregated here looking for shelter—it's not surprising I didn't understand the language that girl and her boyfriend spoke. So many languages, yet, is there just one thing to say. Is that what there is? I fear going on with the writing, but it's a fear that demands I go on. Can one write one's way out of something? Not just out of the fear. Out of the condition.

I organized the Bureau to function as best it could. I applied my trusted, iconoclastic theory of administration: an administrator is not in his job to serve those above him; he is there to serve those below him. That's where his raison d'être comes from. That's where his support comes from. He may lose his head in the process, but he'll keep his mind. His heart. His sleep. Besides, anyone above him who succeeds in getting his head for insubordination, that superior will soon suffer the same fate: his head will roll. I've seen it happen. And who did I have above me? In the Capital there was Garcia. Did she ever read the reports I sent? Did she get them? Did she care? Did she remember that she'd sent me, assigned me? Even though she'd said it was an assignment of primary importance to the Nation, even though she said the assignment had come from above, from the top, even though she'd told me that my wife and daughter weren't incarcerated, they were in protective custody until I finished the assignment, a protective custody they would need because of the enemies my assignment would beget, even so I knew then that my wife and daughter were in prison, that I was exiled.

At first I sat around doing very little except to take notes of my walks. The Bureau existed only to exist. I followed its example. I gave in, so there were many days at the beginning when even the effort to get up to go out for what I called my reconnoitering exercises was an effort beyond me. I could sit in that chair in that office with the fan going overhead (the electricity was still more regular then), I could take a drink now and then, liquor or tea or pure water, I could stare at the walls. Getting up to go out in those days was a defiance of my own inertia. Now, when I go out, there is much too much defeat around me. It is so much larger than any defeat I could ever internally feel, that to go out or not to go out is indifferent. Although I do miss even those early days. How can I say that? How can I look back and find anything there to yearn for? It's just that girl and her boyfriend. I saw them more than once. I saw them often. I subpoenaed them once, but then quashed the subpoena before it reached them. It would destroy what little chance they might have. When was the last time I saw them?

I was out walking. I'll say that a lot in this writing, won't I? I was out walking. When I went out walking it was to find something, always believing I would. That time about six months ago as I walked I saw those two lovers still together. Things were already moving quickly toward what they've now become....I won't call it an end, because something will evolve even out of this. Things move, but not toward ends, only toward difference. Alina was much on my mind.

Alina is often much on my mind. No, Alina is always on my mind. The way the mind works. Something, someone, who is a part of us is then always on our minds in one form or another. The way that both Alina and my wife can be on my mind always. Cohabit that world of what the mind contains, what inhabits it, what world it is in itself. Of itself. The first day that Alina came to me. In my office. That feeling I hated most: the powerful Bureaucrat before the indigent supplicant. The supplicant with no access to the wires of power, believing that I had them, believing they actually existed. I had that feeling mixed in with such an immediate and unnerving desire for her. Not the desire I might feel on seeing a beautiful woman, an interesting woman. Those are all exciting reactions, but active. And in a way my reaction to Alina was—not passive, no, but an active inactivation. It's hard to sift through. The desire I felt for Alina that first minute....it was destabilizing. It sent all the occupants of my own consciousness into an exile where they would have to learn a new order of being. They would all now have to relate in some way to Alina, whom they didn't know at all but who, they intuited immediately, would

SETTLEMENT

become part of each one of them. She had come into the office to find medical aid, remember? Not for herself but for those people who had come with her into the Emergency Settlement from her outlying district.

Alina's town had been completely destroyed in a matter of a few hours by efficient young soldiers, men who moved in command to the voice of a superior officer, a lieutenant or captain; young men who seemed more intent on following the commands of the voice of that superior officer than they were on whatever action they took; young men whose pleasure seemed to be in following that voice, so that they weren't even aware of the destruction they caused, of the chaos, the panic, the suffering they engendered. It had been, Alina said, a beautiful day when they came. Calm and quiet, with the sun quite mildly (in her region the sun can often be brutal) warming the whole town. She told me about it one evening as we lay in bed together. I lay near the window; she lay on her back on the other half of the bed, but quite close to me. She spoke it all out in a dreamy voice, a fluid language as though she were relating something visible but not real. The afternoon breeze came in over my back from the window, cooling. Alina turned to lie on her stomach, her face propped up slightly on the pillow. All the while she talked I ran my hand along the curve of her spine, along the line at the side of her body, where her back and her stomach met, and then, as she turned again, on the near side of her body along that same line. The line that runs from the inside of her underarm to the peak of her hip, over the edge of her buttocks. When my hand arrived mid-calf, it would fall off her body. I would bring it back to where it had begun, just under her shoulder blade, and re-begin that slow journey. She was well aware of my hand. She was even aware of its absence when, after passing the curve of her buttocks, past her thigh and her calf, I would retrieve my hand back up the length of her body without touching her. My hand was connected to her words. The words came from within her, from beneath the skin where my hand traced a course. Her words all came from her breath, from her organs, from the physical memories and sensations of her body. Her words came from the absorbed bodily memories of the attack itself. But those words were so transformed by her body that they came out as the words of a dream, rather than the words of a war. Maybe they even came out as the words of love. I like to think so. Especially now. Especially as I did that day when I went out walking.

It had been a nice day. That was one of the things Alina remembered well, that even in the circumstance of shortages, anxieties about the future, the absence of young men who had been called up in the various drafts, that this Wednesday, when the soldiers had come to her village, it had been, even so, a very nice day. No one suspected anything. The whole town thought that the Government forces were in control of the area. When the soldiers first appeared in a long convoy of trucks and war vehicles, when the citizens first saw the soldiers coming in the distance, it was obvious they were the enemy forces who had broken through the Government lines. But how could that be? Was the Government lying on the television, on the radio, in the newspapers? Had the Government lost control? By the time the troops were near the town, everyone understood that they were enemy troops, as their uniforms and the decor of their vehicles displayed. At first they thought, all right, so now we'll be occupied by the other side for a while.

Alina stopped talking there for a minute. She twirled the forefinger of her right hand on the pillow casing. She followed the line of embroidered linen, then left that line, finger wandering at will. Even though the wind came in cool from the window, still it was warm enough that we had only a light sheet over ourselves. As her finger traced lines about the pillow, my hand ran off the line of its course, traveled over her buttocks, between her legs, which she opened for me as she felt me search for her. Then her body, soft as it was, became tense from the waist. She moved herself toward my hand. What was she thinking as she did that. Was she thinking of the soldiers arriving in her town, or was she thinking of Marcas, her old lover. Or was she thinking of her mother, who'd been killed in the attack. Of her father, who had died of a disease he contracted on their way here, to the Emergency Settlement. She was thinking of something other than me, that was very clear. Except, a minute later, when she turned toward me, when she raised her mouth to mine it was as if in kissing me all those things, the soldiers, her mother, her father, Marcas, all might resolve for a moment into that kiss itself. Who knows?

We lay on that bed so often, talking. So often I lay there, listening. Sometimes now I can hear her words as though she left them here. I try not to let those kinds of things haunt me now. Even this will evolve. I must prepare to accept whatever evolution comes from it. At least I can still hope that Alina is alive. I know that my wife and my daughter are surely dead. They are as dead now as the Government's need of me is dead. That's what kept them alive for a short while. That's what got those letters through. But now that the Government doesn't give a damn about this Emergency Settlement, will let it rot to nothingness, I'm sure that my wife and my daughter are dead. They let them die, they killed them. They would have killed me, too, had I been close enough to them. They knew all along how much I hated them. I was one of the ones who tried to sound a warning early on.

That day I went out walking, it was the end. I mean I must have some way of thinking of it in my own mind. It was the end of my complicity. It was the end of my last breath of hope in survival and recovery under ordinary rule. It was the end of my own belief that I insisted on holding even though I knew it was a complete lie, that the Government still cared about protecting these people here, the people they sent me to help. They never imagined that after the absolute collapse of supplies and aid, after the water stopped coming, after the medicine was long gone, after electricity was a matter of sporadic, momentary surprises, after the Bureaucracy was not only a shambles but a joke to everyone, that I would continue on. I never imagined. I did it not because of my own free will, my noble calling, but because my will had been roused by Alina, by Abanno, by Grammatico. They wouldn't let go. They wouldn't let me go. I wouldn't let them let me go. Perhaps it's absurd. Sure it's absurd. I did it then in a different way, without believing in anything. Maybe if I had come to that earlier I could have saved my wife and my daughter. Or I could have just died with them, I suppose. Well, that's not so bad, is it, to die with your wife and your daughter? The killing of those two, which I know now is done, I mean I know it not just from intuition, although in this case that would suffice. I know it by word that had come to me from friends who were still alive in the Capital. What they must have done to survive these last months. The will to survive. What they must have witnessed there. The decadence. The assassinations. The assaults. The fires. The rapes. I'm sure of it all. It came in their coded words: "Your aunt Sarah sends her regards. All is well." My aunt Sarah died fifteen years ago. Or, "The economy is stable again and we are living as we did." As we did. All we did for the last ten years was live in fear that what has now happened would happen. Or this one: "Your wife's pregnancy failed." My wife wasn't pregnant. That meant my daughter was gone. I hate to say dead. When I was young I hated the hypocrisy of euphemism. I didn't know how I would come to embrace it. She is gone. It suggests she has gone somewhere, is somewhere. It's a trick for the mind to play on oneself, but after all, oneself deserves the favor.

I was thinking about Alina then, that day I went out for that last walk as a Government official. The day it caved in and I gave up. A policeman sat on a curb eating the cooked meat of what looked to me like cat. He stood up when I came near, began even to salute. How long people will carry on a form of living they think might yet save them. He began to salute. I asked him his name, his origin. He told me he came from my neighborhood in the Capital. Where I'd grown up. We talked about that. He'd played in the same places I had, years after I had. He and his friends had played King of the Hill on the same hill where I'd played it, won it, lost it. He'd hidden from his mother's come-in call at night in the same places where I'd hidden. He'd gone to the market for his mother at the same place I had for mine, and the same man, Joshua Louis, still owned the market when the policeman had left to join the service. Now here he was, in my command, a policeman in the Emergency Settlement for the Western Quadrant. I hardly had the nerve to tell him the truth, but of course, I told him. His name was Phillip. I said, Phillip, take off your cap now, and put it away. And when you get home, if you find you still have a home, today, take off your uniform and throw it away. Burn it. Use it for fuel. It's all over, Phillip. That's not an official proclamation. It's unofficial, so you might actually believe it. We've caved in. We've lost. There's nothing for us to do anymore, except what we can invent for ourselves now. I am no longer the Adjutant-General, Civilian Corps, Governor of the Emergency Settlement for the Western Quadrant. I am a man who comes from the same neighborhood you do. Come by some time, we'll have tea together, talk about the old neighborhood. Or, better, tell me where you live now, then I'll come to see you, I'll bring the tea.

Then it rained. I remember that rain by the way it contrasted with the weather Alina had just described to me:

calm and quiet, with the sun quite gracefully warming the whole town. The rain came slowly at first. The skies had been suggestive of rain all afternoon, then it came, while we lay there, while she talked, while my hand ran along her body. Where was my attention most then? On the rain? On my hand? On Alina's body? On the story she was telling me, which I saw so vividly in my mind, my mind adding every detail to her story because I needed to fill it in, to see it. I knew very well that if I turned over I would see rain out the window and not a graceful sunshine, and not soldiers coming nearer from the distance. Rain, ruin. And if I didn't turn over, I would see Alina, her body, my hand, soldiers. Only afterwards, she said, did most of the townspeople—those who had survived—understand that they had been attacked by the soldiers of their own Government. That their town had become a nuisance, or an impediment somehow. How? They marveled at the fact that they had, before the attack, still harbored an axiom of innocence in their calculations. They could not have believed that their own Government would destroy them. Their own people. One of Alina's villagers, a man named Vahid, talked about history, about how this was the last illusion left to civilized history, that a Government would not destroy its own people. Vahid tried to find a way in his thought to redeem humankind even so, to go on with some sense of value or meaning. He wrote about it in a notebook he'd brought with him on the exile. Then he would read to everyone else from the notebook. Notes, poems, historical comparisons, the ideas of religious philosophers. Eventually, before they had reached the Emergency Settlement, Vahid had run out of ink in his pen. Others had, for no purpose they could remember, stuck a pen or two in their pockets, in their knapsacks. Voluntarily they handed them over to Vahid. Anyone who had any thought of writing gave it up, because they wanted to save their ink for Vahid. That was the evening Alina told me about Vahid, it was the evening she told me about everything from before. While it rained, listening to her, I saw the ink of Vahid's notebooks drenched, running into oblivion. It was a strange vision which I never told her about. It's strange to think of it now, because of how I know Vahid now, of how I know his notebooks, of how now I'm writing myself, without hope of being read. I am even tempted to elation by the idea of never being read, as though the writing is in some way and by that fact liberated, utterly free. It's because I've become excessive lately in some of my desires.

I found those three good people already here: Abbano, Tsefud, Rayad. But Tassiossu came later, yes, that's right. I remember the day Tassiossu arrived because he had to come to me for permission to bring all his books into the Settlement. I pretended to examine the books for contraband. What was I pretending, for whom? If I had said right then to everyone present, to Tassiossu, to the guards, to the office workers: look, the man is bringing us books. Praise him. What do we care if they're subversive. All the better if they're subversive. They would have all put down their pretenses right then, taken off their badges, thrown out their identity cards. I had no idea how much I held the center of illusion. I was yet as much afraid of them as they were of me. Such is the way fear works. So here comes Tassiossu with his books, an insane cartage to have hauled all that way. When I opened the first crate I discovered all his books on early Christian art. Only later, in our long discussions late at night in my office, or walking the streets of the Settlement together, did I come to know his obsession with the Madonna. I called on him at first (all of a sudden to think that I am writing this for no one. Why? To recall? To assign all these recollections to an oblivion where I can then imagine they have gone, they are safe, they have become an oblivion that has a certain characteristic, a dimension). When he first arrived with all his books I hoped that Tassiossu would be a scholar, an expert on something. He could lecture us, entertain us, stimulate us, the Bureau, the general population, anyone interested. God knows we needed some kind of activity other than organizing food, water, what little we had or could make or could harvest.

I took Tassiossu on a walk of the Eastern Sector of the Settlement, perhaps my favorite—because it's the oldest. The oldest buildings, what's left of them. Even some small aboriginal dwellings long predating the occupation. Of course Tassiossu didn't trust me then. He thought I was probing for secret political significations or codes in his literature. He was at pains to explain fully, to convince me of the truth of his obsession. I would have believed anything he told me. He didn't know that I believed everyone here, that, uncannily, here no one had ever lied to me. The situation was that desperate even when I arrived, what use was there in lying? Nothing could be more urgent than the truth here. Having not been raised a Christian, Tassiossu had not much regard for what he saw of the Christian world with what he called its obsessive drive for approval, its presumption of guilt, its exculpatory implosions. Coexistent, he said, with that singularly remarkable image of Mary, not as virgin, but as Mother to Christ. Nowhere that he knew of had the particularization of the Mother been so drawn. How so? I asked him. He thought I mistrusted him. He thought I believed he was dissembling, that within these Madonna images, these Great Mother motifs, lay hidden morsels of rebellion, treachery. How could he convince me otherwise?

It's sad for me to look back on this, but everything which arises must be looked back on in order for the whole's assignation to an oblivion of distinction to be accomplished. That which doesn't arise has already found its own form (or formlessness) of oblivion. Poor Tassiossu, gentle Tassiossu, then felt so threatened by my Bureaucratic power that he nearly trembled. If only he could have done what I had already done: in the Settlement, believe everyone in everything they said. Was that another prerogative of power? But I had no power. I had none, and never had any. I knew that. I was a servant. So. In order to convince me of the innocence of his project, Tassiossu told me a personal story, a story too personal to be told to a stranger, a telling which cost Tassiossu a measure of his self-possession. All the unspoken dialogues which went on between the inhabitants and myself in those days. The couple I had seen on the first day, then become so involved with, after quashing their summons. But I'll come back to that. Don't get too distracted, even if this is oblivion's text. Oblivion too has demands of focus, continuity, logic.

So Tassiossu began the story of his life. His own mother abandoning him as a new-born, the hospital which took him in, his days, motherless, as a street urchin, his adoption later, as a young boy, by a prostitute in the City who used him for running errands, her peddling him to men, his escape from her, his love affair with a young girl who, frightened of his petty thievery, betrayed him to the police, his years in prison, the beginnings of his scholarship in prison, his intensifying study, his natural fascination with the figure of the mother in history, of Gaia, of Shakti, of Kali, of Eve, of Lilith. His release from prison and his attempts to gain formal recognition in his scholarship. His embarrassment at disclosing the deep personal need his scholarship revealed was evident in his expression, his manner suddenly shy, hesitant, obtuse, shadowy. Yet he must play this trump card of truth to win conviction from the Adjutant-General, Civilian Corps, of the Emergency Settlement whose protection he now sought. Such an obscure joke.

Nonetheless, without the threat Tassiossu perceived from me I would have lingered for a long time only at the edges of his knowledge, his expoundings on the history of the portrayal of the Madonna, his analyses, probings, comparisons of periodical differences: early Christianity vs. the Middle Ages, the Renaissance vs. the Modern, the Baroque, the scholarly lines of thought entangling knowledge and obscuring the center: Tassiossu's own search for a viable figure in whom to invest his absoluteness. That's how he eventually said it. He was nearly crying that night in my office as we talked. Concrete absoluteness, he said, yet universal connection through a particular figure, or a connection to the universal through its particular aspect. No, he said, I must be mad, that's all. What I mean, he said, is, somewhere to invest the nullity of our absoluteness, that which we cannot spend because it is coinless, but that which, coinless, we must find a way to pay out in order to lighten the weight of it. That's how I understand you now, Tassiossu. After all our discussions. That's how I understand also the turbulence in your work. The necessary resistance we never discussed. I have so many conversations to continue with you.

It was sad then for me to experience the embarrassed price of your intimacy; it was a reward for me to go directly to the motive energy of your vision. I tried, once or twice that evening, to stop him. I tried to indicate nonchalantly that it wouldn't be necessary to open his secret, to grovel. I believe you, I told him, that your interest in the Christian Madonna is an authentic one, not a cover for subversive activity. But circumstances, the times we lived in, the place, wouldn't allow him to trust me. His need to convince me contained his assurance that after he left me he might rest in a little peace, even continue his researches, as much as he could without a library or museum or gallery. Without even a church to visit.

How Alina and I would talk about Tassiossu all that time. Of course, my jealousy. My fear that she would love Tassiossu because he wasn't tainted by power, by association with the Government. She reminded me that I never had power. She would watch my disappointment in her knowledge and tease me, telling me I was like everyone who couldn't forget the self-seducing faith in official power. I would watch my disappointment in her knowledge, and wonder at myself, at how I had come to be such a kaleidoscope of rampant personae.

We hadn't yet met Tassiossu by the night Alina told me the details of the invasion of her village. In the way the psyche organizes time, the invasion of Alina's village became actually an evening in our lives. That invasion was not an event which preceded that evening. It was an event which took place on Alina's face as she spoke about it. The vulnerability which overcame her face when she described her mother's death. That's where her mother's death occurred, in that caution, that softness into which her face devolved as she spoke. By the time her mother was killed, the battle for her village (strange term, she agreed; there was no battle) had been well under way. The soldiers came into the village, so many moving so fast it was hard to distinguish what took place. They must have been expecting an organized defense. They searched out hiding places, cellars, basements, attics, back rooms, culverts, shadowy corners. No one knows why or how the shooting began. Surely, Alina said, no one had shot at the soldiers. Everyone was far too overwhelmed with shock to fight back. She was sure that no one had even absorbed the truth of the matter before the shooting began. Later they all discussed it, on their way here, to the Emergency Settlement. They agreed that probably the first to be shot had been a young man named Rinaldi who'd been shot running out of his house by a soldier who looked like all the soldiers: he was tall, well built, dressed and armed for war. Someone who survived had seen that happen, and all the others agreed it could have been the first killing. Before young Rinaldi hit the ground gunfire exploded everywhere. Soldiers began firing. Alina's face became tense, drawn back. Her body tightened. I felt it with my hand as it went along the curve of her side. I tensed up. She described the sound, erupting from everywhere at once so that it drove you insane, not knowing which way to turn. You were stunned by it, drowned in its attack, the sound-waves attacked your skin. She was hearing the sound of it again as she told it; she wanted to stop it. It was as impossible to stop this time, in telling it, as it had been the first time, in hearing it. Alina became quiet for a minute, the tension holding in her body, in her face. I didn't see them kill my mother, she said. I just saw her lying in the street near our house. She was a strange woman, not always easy. Often difficult, in fact. When Alina said that, her face again relaxed, though her body was still stiffened against the noise of the gunshots. My hand had come to a standstill over her ribs. I watched her so closely. Closing my eyes I saw an odd scene: Alina's mother got up from off the ground to start in on Alina about something or other while Alina was yelling at her to lie back down or she would be killed. I opened my eyes, preferring the reality of Alina's softened features to the ridiculous burlesque of my vision. I asked her why she thought the enemy army found it necessary to kill so many people when no one resisted them. Alina said she didn't think they thought it was necessary, she thought they were doing it for fun. I took my hand off her body and rolled over on my back to stare at the ceiling. I asked her if she loved me. Do you love me, I said. Do you love me? she asked. Yes, I said, yes I do, Alina.

That first evening while I walked with Tassiossu in the Eastern Sector of the Settlement I learned a little bit about his discoveries. About his intriguing mind, his heart that seemed to waver constantly yet possess a directness that would rescue him from abysses too large for him to wander into. The way I might heedlessly wander—for example, into the abyss of the Bureaucracy itself from time to time. The way I would spend days composing memos to heads of Bureaus in the capital addressing the needs of the Settlement, protesting some ruling or other. The way I spent days and weeks trying to get information about our condition to the Capital. I had the older, original residents relate its history, those who remembered it from the days before it became an Emergency Settlement, the names of its mayors, its officials, its police officers. I had them give me figures on crop harvests for various years, then I forwarded those to the Capital, demanding to know why our promised supplies were not coming, why the village had been abandoned to the enemy. I was informed that the enemy had not captured any of our villages, that we had not been abandoned, that the information was mistaken. I would sit in my office at my computer late into the night working on this. My office would become a cell of light those nights. I would become so lost in the work I would imagine the darkness around me obliterated the reality of the last ten years and that only if I stopped work would that old reality be able to reassert itself. I held a vigilance of triumph over circumstances that kept me composing memos to people who probably didn't exist, whose only actuality occurred on the slips of paper I had that listed their names as organizational functionaries. Was I trying to keep Alina from leaving me? Did I already know that she would? Was I hoping my vigils would outlast them, wear them down until they gave me one honest answer, one true reason which I could then take back to Alina as proof that I was doing something worthwhile, that I could connect with the Government, that I could penetrate its miasma to touch its core, proving there was one humane ember worth fanning? Then she would stay with me so that together we could bring the whole thing back to life? Was I just looking for something of value I could bring to her?

Alina admired Tassiossu for reasons I hadn't anticipated. She loved his scholarliness. He held it lightly, without pretense. I arranged for Tassiossu to give lectures, where Alina loved to introduce him. People came, despite the conditions of bad seating, bad lighting, lack of transportation. They walked. Those desert nights with all the stars out. At some of the lectures we were able to provide slight refreshments, tea, bread. A woman we hadn't met before—Lucinda—showed up one evening offering to open the event with a violin solo. She sat in front of the small audience, violin face-down in her lap, bow laid across the back of the violin, without doing anything more. Then she turned the violin over, rightside up on her lap. She sat that way, sat still, not doing anything, doing nothing. We watched her. Then, she spoke.

I can see—she said—that you are not an audience used to the kind of music I am involved in. I prefer to play the potential for music. The possibility of music. Or, if you will, a music which has already been heard, but whose particularity doesn't intrude on the impression of its effect as music. Its impression of musicity itself. Why, then, do I even have a violin with me? This—she held up the instrument—is a violin given to me as a gift by a teacher who believed I could become a musician who would make some contribution to the world of music. I very much appreciated the gesture. If I were here without a violin, the performance would be entirely different. You might say that what I'm playing tonight is the absence of violin. But, oddly enough, without the presence of this violin on my lap, with its accompanying bow, you would not hear the absence of violin which is the totality of violin. What you might hear now is not the violin, it is your expectation for violin music. And that is what I want you to hear. That is the truest music there might ever be. As you can see, without playing, there are several layers of concert, several meanings of performance. Were I to play, I would define only one meaning. I would rob you of the dimensions you can experience in my not playing. Take your expectation home with you. It is equal to all of Beethoven, Scriabin, Tchaikovsky, Brahms, Satie, Monk. Perhaps more real. I appreciate that you are probably not familiar with my practice of music. It is tempting for me to say that to prove my acumen I will come back to play an actual piece for you some other evening. But that would not establish my credibility as a musician, it would diminish it. All I ask is that you not denounce what I'm doing, but think about it. Have a beautiful evening. The potential for music is inestimable, most importantly, it is indestructible, even if all of mankind is destroyed, all creatures with us. Radical times call for radical actions.

What can I say? How can I begin to describe music, even as I am talking to—writing to—a certain aspect of oblivion? How can I describe the effect of that first evening's performance on me? Her virtuosity was evident in her presence. Uncanny. The audience was polite, they agreed to her request, to think about it, though they were not comfortable. I was tongue-tied, embarrassed when I got up to thank her, to introduce Tassiossu. I said, "I don't think that our friend Tassiossu will challenge us to a wordless lecture." When Tassiossu got up to speak, he began: "I am tempted to offer you a wordless lecture. It is already too late." The audience laughed; their discomfort cleared. How many of them truly considered Lucinda's challenge? I hardly did myself, though to some degree I did consider it. I thought about the potential for music as it might occur in Alina's body. I thought about it as it might occur in my wife's and my daughter's deaths, and I must admit that the potential is there, inherent even in those events I can barely stand to think about.

In his lecture that night, Tassiossu talked about one specific rendition of the Madonna and Child. He had discovered in Christian art a difference from the symbology of the Great Mother in other cultures, Kali, for example. The figure of the Madonna embodies no destructive corollary. Tassiossu chose one image in particular, from the third century. He passed around a photograph. Here was the Madonna surrendered to grief, an aspect of her not often seen, but a good one to begin with: its difference even from other Christian portrayals tells us something. It reveals the Madonna's ungodliness. Her powerlessness. Yet, it also reveals a different kind of power: the power to succumb. But that, Tassiossu said, is something gods did not do. They might feel emotion. But they don't succumb to it. In the death of her Child as he is draped across the Madonna's lap in this very early, schematic version with the wood carved almost as a child might draw it, grief so thoroughly invades the Madonna's thin body that it's clear she has no capacity for defense against it, she has no capacity, as a Greek god would, for example, to retaliate. Unadorned acceptance is a radical (the same word Lucinda used) aspect of reality. Thus, he sees in this figure, Tassiossu said, the double-edged blade of Christian life: a desire to portray the mother figure with an inhuman grief, a grief without any counterbalancing anger, irony, bitterness, or humor, suggesting not a powerless mother, but, *au contraire*, an all powerful mother, a mother who can absorb absolutely. This signals, Tassiossu said, such a serious hunger that it might reveal ironically a lack of mothering in the Christian culture, perhaps a fear of or an intense desire for mothering. At the same time, it moves the culture forward toward the possibility of abstraction, the ability to represent with one single thing (in this case one single emotion) what is usually represented with a range of things (a composite of emotion). It seems to me, Tassiossu said, that the crisis which created the Madonna figure in Christian culture always moves backward and forward at the same time. Yet, without a destructive corollary in the mother figure, he asked at the very end of his lecture, isn't there a naiveté to the imagery? Is there a naiveté in the culture? From whence does it arise?

When Alina was telling me about the invasion that evening I had some ideas about my wife and daughter I hadn't thought of before. I saw them, with an intuition which seemed to see more quickly, more vividly, more permanently and with more assurance than usual, that they committed suicide.

Once thought, the possibility confronted me as inevitability. It changed the nature of the music I now associated with my wife's and my daughter's deaths. Lucinda's lecture occurred after the evening Alina told me of the invasion? I'm beginning to forget. No. No. Definitely the violinist's lecture occurred first. But how is that possible if I hadn't yet met Tassiossu? I'm confusing things. I'm sure, though, that once I saw that my wife and daughter committed suicide, I associated a new music with their deaths. I thought of that first the night I lay there listening to Alina. How do I know for sure? Because I remember what Alina was saying. As she recounted the exodus of the survivors from her village the word *exodus* in my mind replaced the word *death*. Death is an exile into which my wife and my daughter had fled. A self-imposed exile accomplished by a suicide which then had a different music attached to it, even though I hadn't attached music to my wife's and my daughter's deaths until I heard the violinist's first concert. Earlier, on the night Alina, in her nearly whispered tone, told me about the destruction of her village, I attached a different music to the suicide of my wife and daughter. Do you follow me? I'm bending time, but that's how it was. You? Follow me? Who? What reader? What self? What other self? Is that who I'm writing for? Another self? Another self of myself? Or just: Other Self?

How mind drifts as it wanders. What terror this can be at times what a deep pleasure at other times.

Alina didn't know how she survived. At one point, a soldier, yelling at her inside her house, leaned into her so close that the spray of his saliva hit her face. Why didn't he kill her? He yelled in a language she didn't understand, but she knew, she said, that his words were double-edged, two-layered: he was telling her to move, to get out of the house, pointing at the front door, while at the same time blocking her way to the door. But the venom of his rage carried another message: he was blaming her for all the evil in the universe, for the violence of this attack itself in which he was caught up as unknowingly, ignorantly, blindly as she was. He waved his gun at her, a metal barrel pelletted with cooling-holes. Shoved her with it. Then he moved aside, shoving her to the door with the tip of the gun-barrel so that he could kill her outside at least. How, she asked me, could those kinds of thoughts have gone through her mind? But they did. A thousand thoughts were running through her, and no thought at all. At the same time. In the sense of a complete awareness of everything around her: the precise physical being of the gun barrel; the solid feel of the wooden door handle; the amount of energy it took to open the door; the difference, visually and viscerally between the light in the house and the light outside; the sound of the door opening; the soldier's saliva spitting out orders to Alina's family. My hand on her thigh. She opened her legs for me to caress the inside of her thigh, then I resumed my usual course along the curve of the side of her body. Her leg twitched when my hand left it. How can I remember all this in such detail? I remember every millimeter of that evening that we lay there. There was much to remember in those days, to keep straight in one's head, first in the City, then here, in the Emergency

Settlement. Who was where, who had done what, what it was permissible to say or talk about, who had been arrested when, who was in hiding, what lies had to be protected, what documents, real or fake, had to be filed where, whom to warn when of what. Now I have the luxury of remembering only what comes to mind, the ease of not questioning whether it is real. Is the memory of my night with Alina, the night she was telling me about the destruction of her village, is it accurate? No matter at all. Her thigh twitched when my hand left it. Yes. This happened. In writing this all out now, for no one, now that it cannot matter any more, each word takes shape around its meaning without stress.

Remember the day Tassiossu broke down crying in my office? I haven't cried for a long time now. I think the last time was when Abanno came up to my apartment with the notes about the water supply. That's when we were still fighting. That's when Abanno was at the heart of things, keeping me going, keeping everyone going. What a character he is. Was he so central to my own ability to go on? Certainly he picked me up from my initial collapse when the Government informed us that there would no longer be any shipments of any kind forthcoming from them. Food. Water. Medicine. Nothing. There were fifteen thousand people here then. Poof. Erase them. How could I have gone on believing they wouldn't do that? Was I just a mass of naiveté? Of continuous unbreakable and innocent hope? Of complicity?

How can I say the Government informed us? They informed me. I was the agent still. I informed everyone else.

I showed Abanno the message first, how it sounded like an order for some insignificant, trivial fact. As though it said "On Tuesday the electricity will be off for one hour for repair at the desert substation." Instead it said "Henceforward, there will be no further shipments of any kind from the Government to the Emergency Settlement in the Western Quadrant." I cabled them: what do you mean 'no shipments'? No food, no medicine? After I got no answer I showed Abanno the original cable. I knew then that I would lose Alina. Isn't that bizarre? I just realize it now in remembering it (and so is it true? Of course it's true. Each word takes shape around its meaning without stress). I knew that Alina would leave the Settlement and I knew that I couldn't. That she wouldn't let me go with her even if I had wanted to. That she would want to go alone, with a few friends from her village.

What kind of man am I? I was Governor for the whole village. I was responsible for them all. Yet when that cable came I cared first about losing Alina. I didn't tell Abanno that because I didn't know it yet. The grief he saw overwhelming me was the grief of losing Alina in the knowledge I was finally admitting to myself that Alina was the last thing I could stand to lose. That's the breach Abanno entered with his determination. His organizational genius that he continued to say was mine, was his. It was Abanno who figured out the rotational water supply systems, making calculations by observing his own water use in detail, then going over old charts of rainfalls, water table depths, maps. It was Abanno who organized the system of runners for communication. Well, I organized it, but it was his idea. I did think of a few things. I came up with the idea for the daily lists of requests from each district. All right, it was Abanno and I together. So many others helped so much, Alina, of course, and her friend, Toby, and then Romero and his crew. But the way Abanno and I kept at it, talking, planning, figuring out, day after day after day after night after day. It wasn't Abanno who did it all, was it? He was as much inspired by my despair as I was by his enthusiasm. I'm just recognizing that. Now life is lived backwards, but the moment of going backwards exists as a revelation of the present. Abanno, there is nothing without you. Strange. I even stopped writing for a minute. Just listened. Heard what? I can't believe I won't see you again, Abanno, that you won't appear somehow, one day just walking in out of the desert carrying some bag of rabbits for a dinner. I detest the will in myself that stops me from feeling absolute despair because of your absence. At the end of so many other absences, my wife and my daughter, my father, faith in the future, in the civic possibility, the absence of Alina. Let the will go. Dissolve into the writing, which too will not forestall something. What is it? I don't know or I don't want to know.

Abanno is the one who introduced us to Meleq. Brought Meleq with him that night we made dinner at my apartment. How normal life could seem. There we were, eating a dinner we had spent two or three hours cooking. There was Alina and Abbano and Meleq and myself. And Meleq, this charming guy, funny. The way he joked about his own dilemma: a writer who had stopped writing when he'd found one page of a novel that he read over and over again each day. The way he made fun of himself, his inability to go on writing until he was satisfied with his reading of that one page. How every day—it was funny, we were laughing so—how every day he read and reread that page imagining that would be the day he would finally know its every dimension. The way he described it, as though the layers in that page were geometrical planes of existence staggered one on the other. He would climb from layer to layer, linger between layers, interconnect them in his own experience, relate words from one layer to words in another layer. How each layer then had its own extension of space at time. In distance. How he would go along one dimension or another exploring it. How it was just as satisfying to read this one page—*Meleq's Page* we had come to call it, or just *the Page*—as it would be to read a hundred books. How, reading the page every day, he would think about it all day differently than the way he'd thought about it any other day. How he felt it important as a writer to be responding to our Emergency Settlement, to the crisis we were all in, his duty even to give us some voice. Every day, all the suffering and all the life around him, every day interacting with everybody who was going through all this, yet all he could do was to read this one page. It was so mystifying to him that he laughed about it. He'd read non-stop, he said, all his life, from the first day he could read even the first letter he learned to read, which he remembered clearly was the letter R. All he did then was to look for the letter R. He'd read and read. And now, he told us, laughing, he'd found this one page, stumbled on it. It was so compelling that he would go back to read it every day, reading nothing else, writing nothing. How could he write, he asked us, until he could know this one page? Then, he said, laughing again, drinking more of the wine we still had in those days, when I've finally absorbed that one page then I'll write, yet what I will write I have no intimation. How we were charmed that night. All of us. Alina and Abanno and Meleq and myself.

And we hadn't even met Meleq's wife yet. What she would have added that night had she been there. What she added later. The way she painted and painted and painted. The less Meleq wrote the more she painted. She was afraid that he would start writing again, she said later, laughing. The way the two of them laughed always. Can it be we led that life? Can it be that I affirm it?

That first night, when his wife wasn't there, Meleq talked about the way he came to her. He called it an underground love. His conscious mind, he said, had not been in love with Rivka when he met her. In fact, it rejected her. But some other part of him, the underground he called it, was in love with her. He followed the underground. His conscious mind never caught up. He learned to disregard it. He laughed when he said that, laughing at himself as though he were some extraordinary creature he had just discovered.

Remember the night Rivka arranged? When Lucinda came with her. She gave another concert just for the four of us: Rivka sitting on the divan, Meleq sitting on the floor leaning up against the ottoman, Alina by the window, me in the easy chair. I see it I hear it. I feel the wind that came in the window that night. Lucinda gave the same concert as her first performance in the Settlement. For a long time, she sat with her violin on her lap, turned face down, the bow laid over the back of it. Eventually, after some time of doing nothing else, quite slowly, she lifted the bow. Very carefully, she turned the violin over, placed the bow across the strings, the strings making the faintest hushed sounds as the bow came to rest against them. Lucinda sat that way for some time. It was the same performance, yet a different one. Was I beginning to understand her? Her concerts were like the one-read page of Meleq's book—layered. Was she managing in our culture—on one layer at least—at the end of our culture, in a society so bereft of vision it had nearly rarefied itself out of existence, had driven itself into an Emergency Settlement, was she restoring the participation of what we call the audience in the act of music? The passive audience into the active community? Because it was a different performance that night. You could only know that by having heard her at least twice. Heard her? Heard yourself. Heard yourself? Heard yourselves: Lucinda, Rivka, Meleq, Alina, me. In that sense it was unrepeatable, wasn't it? It only exists in memory, like now, when I call on it. Why do I associate that evening with the wind coming in the window? Why does wind sometimes make me think of fire? Do I think of fire also when I think of the wind coming in the window over Alina's body the night she told me about the destruction of her village? No. That wind in my memory seems only cooling. It would be fitting if it were associated with fire, but it wasn't, it's not. Fire. Wind/ow. oh fire once dreamt of long ago imagined to cleanse things as though human society were an overgrown forest. Shall I admit what I really heard that night of the second Lucinda concert? The undercurrent of my feelings? The conflicts and the contradictions? The way I desired Rivka, holding my desire for her cradled in my ongoing contact with Alina. As though Rivka were my obscure object of desire. Thinking about Abanno, the way I envied him his enormous capacities. If I could become Abanno. What would I escape, that's what I followed that thought to, paying attention to the wind, listening to Lucinda, if I became Abanno what self would I escape that restricted me? Wondering about the laughter of Rivka and Meleq. Is it genuine? Are they that easy with their own self-sportings? Then thinking, no, I don't want to be as competent as Abanno, I want to be as loose as ironic as playful as Rivka and Meleq who manage to sustain their laughter even here even in the Emergency Settlement. Why am I so serious? Why do I want to be anyone else? What are each of them thinking? Are they thinking that they want to be me for my......what? My whatever. Whatever it is that I can't see. Whatever it is that I am only because of them, only when I'm with them, which I depend on them for being. Why do I compare myself? It's a childish habit. Give it up, I tell myself. Am I too sensitive? Listen to the music, it's interesting what's happening in this room right now. All my thoughts going on and at the same time a web being constructed connecting all five of us not in a silence and I can't say in the music that would be just too easy but in what? Connecting us while separating us at the same time, keeping each one of us at our own junction of the web, our own interchange of connecting lines. How long will she go on with this? What is she thinking, Lucinda? I'd love to be a musician, like her, to be so engrossed in music all the time. Is she thinking is she hearing some actual music? I'm not. I'm just hearing what's here. Myself. Them. And even though we breathe the air that comes in on the wind, the wind is a separate thing. I wish she would play something. I would love to hear the sound of that violin. This is agony. It's coy. Yet the absence of the music —the potential music absorbs it all that's the thing. Absorbs all my thoughts all theirs. Will Alina stay with me? I don't think so somehow. I will lose her yet I don't know why. Why? Because ever since my wife and my daughter (I'll always call them that from now on not by their names but my wife and my daughter I will refer to them in my mind in their primary relationships to me because it's my way of keeping them primary and at the now necessary distance at the same time) committed suicide everything which happens is temporary? No, it's not happening. I'm not in this room with this woman playing her counter-violin her alter-violin her ulterior-violin her true-violin her violinless-violin with Rivka with Meleq with Alina. They're wonderful these people here. I wish Abanno were here tonight. Why didn't I invite him? Stupid of me.

Now that's strange. I was in a trance for a while writing that. I went back there, to that evening. Before Meleq got up to read us *the Page* that had completely absorbed his creative mind. He sat down on the same chair Lucinda had sat in, opened the book, put it face down on his lap. We laughed, but he kept it up. He sat there for a long time until we knew he wasn't just joking. Then he turned the book over, open on his lap. What an urgency that created. We wanted to hear those words now exposed. The words wanted to be read. But after a while everyone relaxed, I mean that I did and the words did. Well, that's crazy, but there's nothing to fear anymore, not even craziness. So what if I go crazy? Write what you like. Yes? The words did relax. Their anxiety to be heard relaxed. They laughed at themselves a bit, at their zeal to be known orally, out loud, to show off. Everything was alright and they relaxed. They became part of the the-music-the-non-music-the-silence-as-music. They were the libretto. See, I can say anything now because no one will read this. You can say anything now because no one will read this. It is a complete secret. You are writing finally. You amuse me. You remind me of a schoolboy told that he must write a certain way, while inside him he wants to write another way. Yet he so wants to please, to do it right, to be what the teacher wants him to be. He's a good boy. It's alright. He can write whatever he wants to now. For quite a while Meleq had that smile on his face. Then it softened. He just sat there. He could have been holding any book at all.

Now you can go anywhere you want. Within the realm of the Emergency Settlement, now that the Emergency Settlement is your only world. It has been ever since you arrived, but you didn't realize it yet. Like the walk you took on your first day here. Remember? You should have known because that was the day you first saw Ibrahim. No. That's the one thing I don't want to write, don't want to walk back into. You can write anything you want; I also grant you permission not to write what you want to efface. Is that cowardly? Isn't the whole idea to write into exhaustion every thing there is to write? No. Then what is the point? Point? Of the writing, don't lose concentration, the point of the writing. Is the point of the writing separate from the act of the writing? Pursue that. Think about it. Can you think? While writing? Isn't the writing stronger than thinking? Doesn't it replace thinking for you? Perhaps I write for the joy of writing and that's it. Joy which we would like to cohere into something like meaning is the joy of writing a mask over something more significant when in fact the mask is the surface is the sum fullness of it all. We see a face—Guillemette, say—we know that behind that face a world a universe we call consciousness exists. But we can't apply that mask/face/consciousness as analogy to the surface of things in general. The joy. The page. Here I stop writing. I sit back like a man relaxing in the sun in a piazza to blankly, simply, in a curious kind of adoration take in the world strolling by. Even though here only silence and absence stroll. I lean back. Now. Go back to the girl and the boy. Write of them. With their one paper coffee cup between them. Laughing. Remember how you would see them often after that first walk. Or remember the day you went with Alina to Meleq's, so he could actually read you *the Page* he'd been reading every day. Or remember Alina lying in bed talking to you about the attack on her village. You were tracing your hand along the curve of her body. The wind was coming in from the window, blowing over you and her, cooling you. There is a danger of running out of ink before everything is finished. It all seems finished, yet there's a storehouse of ink left. You have to exhaust the ink, too, not just the impulse to compose. What is it you're trying to say? Talk about Meleq, about going to Meleq's with Alina. Or, hell, talk about Ibrahim if you want. OK, Meleq. There's a story in it, irresistible to your pen, right? Do I detect a note of hostility toward yourself? All right, Meleq.

It was because of Alina. She wanted to visit Meleq. Was this after the night she lay in bed telling you about the attack on her village? Yes, it must have been, because on the walk over to Meleq's she mentioned the attack again. She brought up the question of why she hadn't been killed. The soldier on the porch of her house. All the soldiers with their hyped-up ferocity. But, she said, it was an impersonal fury, featureless, cold. Without satisfaction for them. The soldiers were as afraid or even more afraid than she or the villagers were; in killing the villagers they were killing their fear they were becoming blank. It was one of those moments with Alina….I could have said that she wasn't killed, that she was spared so that later we could meet. The kind of thing you would say to redeem an unredeemable event. But saying it here would imply that we might have gone on, Alina and I. Or that the soldiers, they had stepped outside of their own wrath in order to annihilate the village. In order to make its annihilation completely meaningless. She was becoming agitated. I sat her down on a rock by the side of the road. I calmed her by telling her about the first concert that Lucinda gave. Why hadn't Alina ever been as shaken by her memories as she was that day, walking on the road? She wasn't exactly calm the first night she told me. There was a calm in the room, perhaps. There was my hand going up and down the edges of her body. The incredible stories! Even I, I have seen of a lot of hell. Even I, when I think about it, of course, I'm horror stricken. Even now, writing it again. For the last time now? Why wasn't I more agitated that first night she told me? Because I was so glad just to feel her voice, the tone of intimacy drawing me into her. The pleasure of sharing in the abjectness of her sorrow. A safer projection of my own horrors. Possible to endure in the other what each couldn't endure in themselves. To whom, then, am I speaking now? To what other? Alina? None. That's the important essential crucial indispensable imperative vital fact of this writing by which it exists.

That rock Alina sat on that day. By the roadside. Grey. Thigh-high. Rounded with its flattened table. How did it get that shape, by what history, and how did it get to be there, by the side of the road? Her legs dangled over the edge of it. Her hands behind her at first supporting her torso in a triangulation, the rock taking the weight of her body, the pressure of her hands down against it. And then me, wandering away from the rock, then pulled back to it. Pacing around it. Not altogether grey. With some white lines in it, some black spots. How it seems to have a meaningless presence, serve no function. Yet its presence is all that much stronger. Meaning detracts then from presence. Function detracts then from form. The first law and the first corollary of this writing? The first writing after the end of the Emergency Settlement of the Western Quadrant and all that went with it? Nearly the end. And the end of what else we who have now lived here out of contact for so long, we don't know what else has ended. Alina sat on the rock while I recalled Lucinda's first concert to her. After a while, Alina calmed down.

Who am I writing to? To whom? The whole history of literature and its audience, an acrobatics of the image and the word. The idea. Are there others like me now composing out of no discernable motive, notes in the first person like a narrative? In the second person as though I needed some other self with which to discuss it all? So I in him. You invent him. Second person familiar. I'm the audience. No, "you" are the audience. No. There is no more audience. I accept it. I feel like I've come full circle, writing on parchment, on stone, on a cave wall, spitting pigment, carefully, intently, over my outspread hand.

They were from the south, remember? Oh, I remember very well. I remember most vividly the sprockets the chains on their machines. Why do I go on to describe them as though I were writing for even one person? My own memory is sufficiently raised by just a mention of them. I write for the page now, for some abstract thing called "the narrative". I write for the joy of memory. Guillemette first came to my office requesting permission to do the performance publicly. Sitting on the other side of my desk she drew sketches of their machines. "Macchine," she called them, "macchine antiche."

Machines as old as the story her group of machinists/actors would tell. Big machines, ten, twelve feet tall, on inch-wide wooden wheels, with low bicycle seats on which a machinist/actor would sit peddling the huge contraption into the middle of the Old Square. The biggest machine, with intertwined chains and pulleys, would require three machine-operator/actors/pedlars. And each machine, with its round wheels, its cranks pulleys bicycle chains would support an over-sized enormous fairy-tale sized construction of an insect made of wire and colorful papers.

Guillemette drew diagrams of each machine/insect. Red green yellow orange insects. Another machine would have a platform at the top with an actress on it.

Asking my permission! Artists asking the Bureaucrat's permission to fulfill their vision at a time in history when Bureaucracy was already a heap of tepid ashes, if anyone would only look at it. I assumed my role. I examined her drawings. I asked questions. Then formally I formally granted her official permission with the full-hearted support of the entire Department, the whole Government-In-Extremis.

Guillemette kept me apprised throughout the two months of building the insect machines. The pilfering of metal, steel, wood. For all of which I signed documents of permission. Abanno made beautiful fakes for me. I signed them, gave them to Guillemette, told her to use them freely. She offered to dedicate the performance to me, "The Enlightened High Prince of the Emergency Settlement" she dubbed me. Looking back on it now I think I was right not to disillusion her, not to abandon my post simply because I knew it no longer existed. I delighted in issuing fabricated requisition slips for scraps and equipment the Gruppo delle Macchine del Ferro could have stolen from unguarded heaps, bought on the black market, found in abandoned houses without any permission from my office. With these requisition papers—were they fake? I did sign them. I was head of the Department. Of course they were fake. Completely—with these requisition forms the performance had already begun. Each ceremonial presentation of false documents to Guillemette a short act in the drama. A comedy farce as though each time my face were painted an absurd bright exaggeration. Thus I became a member of the Gruppo delle Macchine Viventi and thus I performed the only Bureaucratic acts which ever gave me pleasure and thus I the Bureaucrat learned that all pleasure partakes of madness, pantomime, silliness, transgression, and the validation of the seemingly false which is actually not the true false.

The performance took place on a sunny day. They had filled the square with the great huge flapping awkward clumsy machinery of the Fly, the Butterfly, the Garden of Flowers (high up on a platform the machine supported), the reddish-brownish-bluish Dinosaur-Beast, two smaller Dinosaur-Cohorts, the Spider, the huge Spider-Web woven of thin rope, atop another machine—a platform with a bed—and all these machines on wheels. For some of the machines they made rubber wheels to replace the wooden ones —where did they find rubber for wheels!

Yet, the first thing I noticed when I came into the square

was a little boy in a yellow jumper chasing groups of pigeons. He neither smiled nor grimaced nor laughed; he was absorbed in his childish pursuit without a strain in his face.

The members of the Gruppo delle Macchine Imaginary milled around their machines. Alina found me in the crowd. Throughout the performance she held my arm, even though I ran around the square with the crowd, following one machine or another.

Music came from loudspeakers. They had loudspeakers!

Grammatico pedaled out the first machine: the platform high up with Guillemette on top, in a bed asleep. He pedaled his contraption around the square, gears and chains rolling. They hadn't tried to hide the actors/machinists/ pedlars. They weren't costumed. The rough apparatus of the drama was bared. It was theater. The crowd applauded, running to get out of the way of the oncoming great machine, while still hovering as close to it as they could. On the platform high atop the machine, Guillemette awoke in her bed. She stretched. She took in the day. She was a Child awakening from Child's Bed. Everything she saw delighted her. She yawned giggled stretched. The music played on. The crowd followed. T-shirted, Grammatico worked at the big flat pedals, rolling the wooden-wheeled machine over the cobbled square. Guillemette looked up at the sky, sighed like a Child, clasped her hands to her breast. (It was even better that Guillemette was in her early fifties, making no effort to hide the age in her face with make-up. She wore a young girl's bed-clothes, she held a rag doll in her hand, but otherwise, like the machines, she did not hide the flesh the human machinery of theater. Grammatico pedaled the machine past the flower-garden (wooden Petunias, Cosmos, Lavender on great 5-foot tall stems surrounded by leaves of green grass—where did the paint come from?). In exaggerated gestures Guillemette inhaled the flowering scents, threw out her arms as if to embrace the Garden in whole in her Child's bosom. Grammatico kept her moving. She sighed. She laughed. The crowd followed her. Bravo! Applause! Delight!

Klaus, from the sidelines, pedaled out his machine into the scene. The Fly. Up in the air, it swiped by Guillemette, she swiped it away. It buzzed her, she shooed it off. It flew around, the crowd flailing to shoo it off when it came near them. Then Khoffí came in fast on his contraption: The Bee. The music turned dark, threatening. (Where did they get their music?) Khoffí pedaled quickly toward the circling platform-bed while Guillemette flailed her arms around, fending off the danger until the Bee discovered the garden, where it hummed in ecstasy among the flowers among the euphoric odors, delirious, happy in the dew wet in the pollen sweet light soft. The music became bucolic—one flute.

By the time the crowd heard Atthonis howl his first fierce cry, turned to see him enter the square, he had already taken a good head start from aways back. Here he came, not sitting but standing, pedaling, shouting great cries deep groans his face red-flushed with passion with fury unbound. His hands gripped the metal tubes of his machine, shaking them so that the Spider atop Atthohis' machine trembled while its Spider legs rose and fell climbing the air, the bed, Guillemette's head, on toward the Fly which it herded to the Spider's web but didn't stop no it turned with renewed bloodfed purpose to the garden to fill its greed to force the bee through the clustered flowers out into the open then drove it toward the web where the Fly, struggling, entangled profoundly while Atthonis yelled screamed drove pedaled shook while the crowd, silenced, followed the machines of this lyric turned epic while the music became rhythmic, strong-accent-beated.

The Spider devoured the Fly along with the trapped Bee, those insects collapsing by the gathering in of pulleys, strings, folding wings and legs, then withdrawing from the scene, all the while poor innocent Guillemette screamed in her best little-girl's high-pitched helpless voice while no one came to her aid while the crowd ran around the square wanting to strike out at the Spider but not.

Guillemette collapsed in tears and defeat. Sobbed. The crowd became limp. Grammatico slowed the pace of his circling cycle. The chains ground audibly around the gear-wheels. Could the Gruppo delle Macchine Fantasmagorie cloud the sky with darkness they would have. The skies stayed clear, white and blue. I wanted heavy cumulistic gloom to move in; I wanted to see that the Gruppo delle Macchine Famose could organize truly the wind and the rain, the clouds, the skies, the light and dark of the earth in her atmosphere. I wanted desperately for that transformation to be possible, to be effected by my friends in the Gruppo delle Macchine Terribili. I wanted a change at the very core of Universal Order, didn't I? Nothing in the atmosphere changed. Amid the chaos of the machines rolling over the plaza, the noise of the crowd in appreciation, delight, fear, the screaming of the Child-Guillemette up on her platform-bed, the violence of the Spider/Fly-Bee battle, I stood amid the riot of my own desires aroused, and so standing and watching, I noticed in fact a preternatural stillness in the air, the temperature, the foliage around us, the light, as though the universe did respond by command of the Gruppo delle Macchine Supernaturale by precisely its stillness into which even the growth of plant or tree or grass of herb was incorporated.

Guillemette wept, the crowd (and not the sky) darkened, slowing with the slowed pace of Grammatico's peddling. Standing still there I succumbed to a panic, a fear which became a terror — of abandonment, of aloneness at that moment when my actual breath changed pace and depth I in some way lost what I call consciousness which is what, really? A sense of connection to others? A sense of purpose, motivation? A sense of time? A sense of place? But succumbing to the terror was pleasure, release by some obtuse osmosis of my own terror into the stillness of that moment. Now, here, I am alone, abandoned, alone. Without purpose, nearly loosed from time. And? Now, as I write, the sensation of that terror seems a luxury I wish I could retrieve.

As Guillemette recovered from her grief three actors/pedlars: Angela, Rahad, and Simond—coordinating their labors—brought forward the Dragon-machine. This red-blue-purple Beast had claws each half the size of my body.

Guillemette summoned it, it rolled forward to her

command. Now two others in the Troupe, Hwang and Samson, came out onto the plaza to yell orders at the pedlars, guide their machines, direct the oncoming action.

As the Beast approached Child-Guillemette she became the Queen of the Underworld, the Goddess of Vengeance, the Sword of Truth. The Beast fawned on her, she rubbed its flanks, snout, neck. She raised her arms over the Beast, her eyes enlarging, her mouth turned, and by the Power vested in her by Primordial Innocence, she blessed the Beast with the blessing it hungered for. She sent it off into battle.

The Beast's two lizardy underlings attacked the Spider from back and front, claws and teeth, talons, body thrusts. Within minutes the enormous Spider had shredded them, dropped them to the ground, their weight felling the two actors, Michealis and Hequetor, under them. Hwang and Samson, the ground crew, rushed over to unstrap the gear, Michealis and Hequetor slipping out, then the four of them carried the sub-Beasts off the plaza.

In the chaos of this death the Spider had disappeared, but to return with another howling rush from off-stage as Atthonis pedaled like a mad-man from Hell, the Great Spider shaking, raging. The battle of the Beast and the Spider took place all over the plaza. Back and forth. Round. Four people peddling and manipulating their Macchine with primal animus. All joy or comfort or sweetness banished from earth. Guillemette shouted on her Favorite, her Beast, dancing slow-limbed big-arched movements in the glory of bestial power. The crowd, standing back away, watched from a circle which broke around the plaza as the two Creatures threatened to come near.

Until the Spider, over-reaching, stretching his neck, exposed it.

In one move the Beast bit with his down-swooping teeth.

The spider's severed head smashed to the ground.

Atthonis accomplished this with latches on strings. He pedaled back, then forth, then slowly, slowly backwards until gone. Beside the square, out of the action, Atthonis sat in the crude driver's seat of his once fierce now beheaded Spider-Machine.

Bravo! Bravo! Bravo! (Was it Bravo! the vanquishing of the Spider or Bravo! the adroit performance of the Gruppo delle Machine Surrealistice) It was not the same crowd who had given applause and approval and open-hearted delighted hopeful enthusiasm to the first appearance of the clumsy colorful machines. It was a crowd now moved by a different overpowering emotion.

The music, bassic, turned colorful, pianistic, complex lyrically, rhythmically. Guillemette, pedaled by Grammatico, circled the plaza with the garden circling around her. The Beast approached Guillemette, who bowed her gratitude, kissed the Beast's cheeks, knighted him with the invisible medals of her now-gracious sovereignty. The hegemony of peace drew the crowd's new applause.

There. Narrative is served, completed. Achieved. Formed. Afterwards, walking home alone through the emptied square I saw the couple again, the boy and girl from my first day. They were on a bench, kissing. They were drunk, or seemed drunk to me. I'm sure they were. They were all over each other in self-abandoned lust. Groping, entangled, licking, kicking. They were lost, two wild teenagers anxious to destroy by scorn by the embrace of disillusionment the whole construct of the adult world, its rules, compromises, its hypocrisies, its possibilities for meaning.

Crossing the square emptied except for the drunken lovers I sat for a minute on a bench. Strange how the mind works on its own. I saw in an afterimage the small boy in the yellow jumper with the simple look of concentration on his face chasing pigeons as they flew away. There was a time I would try to interpret that image as though it had come to mind for some reason. Interpretation is a luxury of a more civilized leisure. Now I just see the image, the full seeing of it the only interpretation it permits me. And yet, now I know: seeing it is the complete and full and fulfilling interpretation of every image.

I went home to change before going out to look for Alina, who had disappeared into the crowd. I didn't realize she actually had gone off until after the performance when I couldn't find her. Swept up into that celebration into which Guillemette and the Gruppo drew me—The Englighened Prince of The Emergency Settlement, they called me, His Most Bountiful Beneficence, His Excelling Excellence, and so on as they reveled—I glanced around for Alina.

Admit it. After that, you knew Alina was gone, didn't you? Why after that? How many times do you have to ask that question of yourself until you know that you'll not be able to answer it? Was it something in the production of The Gruppo delle Fiore Esegerate that drove her away? Was it something of your involvement with the Gruppo delle Imaginazione della Vita that did it? My most real question: how did I know that Alina would leave after that? When she didn't say anything. Suggest anything. How, sometimes, we read each other without knowing we are even doing it, our own responses to the readings often so deeply unarticulated to ourselves that we couldn't possibly say anything to the other, or act, until much later. What was I picking up from Alina in my fingers the night she told me of the invasion of her village? As my hand wandered the length of her body. As she talked about the soldier holding her at bay on the porch of their house as her parents and her older sister and her two brothers were dragged out by eight other soldiers who took them off. She had counted them. Why had she done that? she asked me. Seeing each one of their individual faces she had given it a number. One. Two. Three. Four. Five. Six. Seven. Eight. Then, after they were gone, the soldier holding her, the ninth soldier—though she hadn't yet given him that number —something had shaken him, startled him, shocked him, something which had not come only from the events in front of his eyes, something which came into him from memory, or idea, or recognition, or awakening. Facing her, his words came straight from his body without thought: "You!" he said, "yes, you." To him, at that immediate moment of chaos, she was responsible for whatever recognition he had, or she was the object of his recognition, or she had initiated all the horror around them, or he recognized her as something or someone to which he had long been blind, and he now just now in the chaos of the immediacy of this moment he recognized her, realized her. That voice of his saying "yes, you, you." It was a stream that poured into her body from his. I ran my hand along her thigh, so well-known to me. I felt to see if I could discern remnant tracings of that soldier's voice. Either it was gone — dissolved into her or out of her—or I was insensitive to it. I wanted it as a ritual of communion between us. As a mutual cleansing. Maybe, with all my experience of the world, I am too innocent to perceive such a thing. That's entirely possible. Although the soldier's voice was hot, she said, her body through fear froze it. He didn't attack her then, he didn't hit her, shoot her, slap her, stab her with his bayonet. Paralyzed with ambivalence, he faced her. Then he ran away, leaving her on the porch, she said, although later she changed that story.

That's why Meleq was reading *the Page* of fiction over and over. So the story wouldn't change. No, he was doing it because each time he read it the story changed, it was an endless story contained in one story, one *Page*. What a genius, Meleq! You discovered something. Why that *Page*? I never looked it up. You told me what book what page number but I never wrote it down. It's here, among what's left. I'll pour through your books now, trying to guess what *Page* it was. And then what will I know, if I find it? Will I know you, Meleq? Is that what I'll find there if I read it over and over, the way you did. Will I find some answer to all this. Will it comfort me. Will it obviate the need for comfort by the action of contemplation. Will

I find out why I go on with this writing. As if I could ever guess which *Page* it was. Yes, I could guess. If I look carefully and with an open concentration through the right book *the Page* will become obvious to me. I'll know it for sure. This is something like Lucinda's violin concerts, isn't it? I will create the reading you left for me, as I hear the music she left here.

In a way it's like Tassiossu's dilemma of the Madonna. At first Tassiossu compared the Madonna to the mother figure, the Great Mother so ubiquitous in all cultures. Yet the Madonna represented an aberration in world culture, Tassiossu said, which required investigation. It must signify a rupture in Christian culture, a crisis of mothering, a loss of knowledge about mothering, wherein the culture had to frantically externalize, objectify such a figure. This didn't quite fit with the best theories of symbol, image, or myth. But what Tassiossu saw of the products of Christian culture signaled to him that something at the core of it was amiss. Something so overdrawn as to be anxiety-ridden about it. Tassiossu admitted that only as an outsider might he have noticed that, that it may exist in his own culture also but hidden from him. Just the point, he said. For better or worse, he said, I can study Christian culture in a way I can't study my own. I am an anthropologist who views Christian society as the object of study. What can it reveal to us about ourselves? I protested. I'm a Christian, I said. I don't want to be studied. Don't worry, he told me, I'll bring you yourself signified, I'll present you to yourself so you might understand who you are and how you got to be here. Through your study of the Madonna? I asked him. Exactly, he said, all I need is one image to begin with to recreate the whole creature. That image happens to be, he continued, a scraping right off the central nervous system. Your central nervous system! I told him. Well, he agreed, yes, the central nervous system of the whole universe was indistinguishable in its parts from the whole. And, he added, it was exactly because this image of the Madonna represented a powerful crisis, an essential anomaly in the culture, could he use it so effectively to describe the culture. A powerful crisis in *your* [how good I'm getting at italics!] life! I protested. He answered me by saying that the closer his non-Christian soul was to the elemental quest of Christianity the more vibrant an observer he was.

I told him then about my dream, that I had dreamt of the *Pieta* he had showed and talked about the night of his first lecture, the wooden one, thin figured. In the dream, he, Tassiossu, was the figure of Christ who lay wounded and dying in the lap of the Madonna. All his researches, I told him, were an investigation into his own desires. He wanted to lie in the lap of the Madonna, I told him, to feel the absoluteness the totality even the oneness of the Madonna's love and sorrow. He wasn't studying Christianity, he was studying himself, Tassiossu.

That's when he told me about the lie. He had lied to me the first night we met. His mother had not died when Tassiossu was a child, leaving him orphaned. His mother had been a wonderful woman, actually, very loving, very lovely, he had many fond memories of her, deep attachments to her. He had told me the lie because he didn't trust me. He thought he had to convince me that his researches came out of some deep trauma in himself, that they were personal, not subversive. He was trying to save his skin and his books.

But why *that* lie?

Because it's the lie that makes the most sense, he said. Those things could have happened to me. I know what they would mean. They are happening right now to someone. Is it me? Is it not me?

Then it's not Christian culture you're so interested in? I said.

Yes it is, he said. Christian culture represents this obsession more adamantly than any other. More vividly. More historically. It can be so clearly traced through centuries of art and literature.

But what about other cultures, I asked him. What about Hinduism? What about Kali? I knew nothing about Kali then. How I even knew her name to throw at him I don't know. When had I ever studied Hinduism? Never. Things, seeping from culture to culture, become common. The cultures surrounding us, the culture that Alina comes from, the culture that Meleq and Rivka come from. Cultures that—as an officer of the Government—I should know. Oh, he got excited, then, Tassiossu did. Yes! he said, yes. Exactly Kali. The perfect counterpart. Kali, Tassiossu said, has three aspects: Creator, Preserver, Destroyer. Wearing a garland of skulls, an upraised sword and a severed head in her hands, she dances in the midst of destruction. Kali gives birth; Kali preserves vitality;

Kali takes life. This is the ambiguous multibiguous vision. The Madonna is singular: She is pure love. Pure suffering. Kali doesn't suffer the death of her children. She creates their death. Your Christian Madonna, Tassiossu said, is an under/god, a demi-god, for she suffers the death of her son. This is either—here, he told me, is the crux of my researches—he got very clear-headed, spoke distinctly, each word enunciated. This...Christian...iconography...represents...either a step forward...into a notion...of pure...universal...love...or a step...over the line...into trashy...sentimentality. He laughed. Worse, he said, laughing his words, flinging his arms around. Delusional distractions, wayward paths. One day I think it is one way, the next day I think it is the other way. They both fascinate me. I pour over renditions of the Madonna. I like the stick-figured one I used in my lecture and which came up in your dream, he said. It is so very old, from the 3rd century, done with such primitive materials, not even wood, really, but sticks, raw. It embodies that new Madonna so profoundly: simple suffering. Human agony. A capacity absent from Kali; a delusion irrelevant to Kali.

Do you see? His excitement had grown so that he spoke with more conviction and more confusion at the same time. Do you see? he said. Kali represents an understanding in Hindu culture of the nature of the universe, or, he said, the Universe, if you like, capital U. The Madonna represents a lack of understanding of the Universe. It presents a figure of protest. Kali presents a figure of acceptance. And yet, the acceptance of Kali—and here's where things get turned on their head—the acceptance in Hindu culture of life and death could be ersatz compared to this almost laughable innocence of the Madonna, because with the Madonna as a suffering human creature, the culture admits that it knows nothing about the workings of the Universe. An admission not often recognized, perhaps even only latent. The acknowledgment of that unknowing might be a more sophisticated posture. Do you see?

I did see. My conversations with Tassiossu from then on were almost always about his researches. All those images he brought for me to look at. All that talk about Kali/Madonna/ Great Mother/Gaia. I don't complain. It was so intriguing. How I loved (love) Tassiossu! Perhaps most of all because in his researches there was a terrible and a wonderful aspect of loneliness and communion. Here was a man, my friend Tassiossu, searching among the fingerprints of cultures for evidence of something inside himself. That's what I said to him. I said, Tassiossu, despite your disclaimers, despite the fact that you are a foreigner to the Christian world, you're looking for something inside yourself in these Madonnas. I may not know what it is, I may speculate, but surely that's what you're doing.

Oh, yes. Finally he agreed. Oh, yes, he said to me one day, that was about 4 months ago. We were out walking. By then we both knew that things were deteriorating yet we talked about it only briefly. We passed by that donkey dead in the street. That's not just a dead donkey, I said, it's a bad sign. I know it, Tassiossu said. Believe me, he said, I know where we're headed. I'm trying not to let that happen, I told him, and it was true. I was trying then. I believed we could stem it. That was about the time the fighting came so close to us for a while. We heard it that day. Tassiossu would identify artillery from its sound. That was the day that Empouche found us walking. He was wild. Hysterical. Still in the tatters of a uniform. Up against that wall you motherfucking sonsabitches up up put up your hands against the wall don't fucking move. You lackey fucking bastards. Identify yourselves. Fucking identify yourselves! Who the hell are you? Who the hell are you? Tassiossu asked him. I was too scared to blink. Tassiossu so damned cool. Empouche answered him: I'm the one with the fucking gun, right? All right? Tassiossu said, and we're the ones without the fucking guns. All right? Somehow that disarmed Empouche. Well, not literally. Well, literally. It made him think.

So I said to Tassiossu...well, later. Should I stop writing here to put in the story of Empouche, how he arrived here, what happened? For whom? I know the story of Empouche. Tassiossu knows the story of Empouche. Alina certainly knows the story of Empouche. Is the fact that there will be no reader a liberation? I never thought of that, that's for sure. I thought of it only as a despair. A loss I've known all along. At times even that no-one-who-will-never-read-this has become a person in my mind so funny the mind is. Dear No-one, do you need me to fill you in on the story of Empouche, how he got here to live with us? Can I assume you know it? That it's one more story, all of which you already know? Can I go on with my story of Tassiossu? I can go on? Thank you.

That was the day Tassiossu admitted he was looking

for something inside himself. That the lie he told me on the day we first met was not an autobiographical lie but a psychograpical truth of sorts. Yes, he said, I want to lie in the lap of the Madonna of Christian culture, as I see her in all those representations. I want to feel the release of my chest, my mind, my heart being held so lightly, so abundantly. I want to feel all grief, even deep, secret grief I can't touch, don't even know, absorbed into her body, that body of the Madonna I see in artists like Giotto, Parmigianino, Scroffut.

Are you so very alone? I asked him. So abandoned?

Aren't you? he asked me.

I almost said no, didn't I? I almost said, no, I'm not, I'm a Bureaucrat who believes in his work and those whom he serves and the future. Fortunately, before those words came out I knew how foolish how small how mundane they were. Yet now I see them otherwise. Well, isn't that interesting? Now whom are you writing for? To enlighten yourself? What I said to Tassiossu was: how can you be so absorbed in such a pursuit in the midst of all that's happened to us in the last year, in the last five years? Aren't you moved to do something? Aren't you compelled by the urgency around us?

Isn't what I've just told you an urgency? Tassiossu asked me. My researches, he said, aren't they a large urgency? Maybe I'm beginning to understand him. I don't think I did before everything collapsed. I tried to. But I tried to convince him, too, that we could change things. That we could at least help those who needed us, help ourselves. Tell me what to do, Tassiossu said. Tell me where you need me and I'm yours.

These are not mutually exclusive pursuits, he said, my pursuit of the Madonna and your pursuit of…what? he said. I don't know really what you pursue.

If you want to help, I told Tassiossu, continue to lecture on your researches. It's an important contribution, I told him. Even in the midst of the fallen donkey, even if we were headed for catastrophe. As it has happened. I was right, wasn't I? I at least helped keep us alive, in more than one sense. Alive. Didn't I? That's also when Tassiossu's work with Empouche began, well, not long after that.

Dear reader, I address myself. I address myself to you. The stakes now are deeper, yet less important. That's the paradox. That is, not less important, no, less useful, no, not less useful, no, less…but maybe not deeper at all. Is it deeper? Deeper than what? Before? Not deeper than before, not less important. Just deeper, more significant, less important. Deeper than ever! Deeper than ever. Deeper. Not deeper. Different. How different? Not different. Not the same.

When she told me that how did I feel? Many different things at once. Looking back on it now it's hard. My feelings have changed. You can never say how you felt at some time in the past. What you can say is how you feel now, remembering what happened then, or what you think you felt then. Or might have felt. What she, Alina felt. What did Alina feel telling me about it? That's a more complex question even. What did Alina feel remembering it, recounting it to me? What did she feel doing it? Why did she do it? Does that matter? She did it. She took him to her, the Ninth Solider. She kissed him. Held him to her kissing him with her eyes closed with herself lost in that kiss for a minute, two minutes, three minutes. Then she opened her eyes to meet his eyes, opened. She never even ended it. He did, he ended it then only because he might be caught. While her father, mother, sister, two brothers were… whatever. She was the one who led the whole village here. Was it from the strength of that kiss that she led them? "I was a dead woman kissing a dead man," she said. Or a woman lost kissing a lost man. Or a simple woman kissing an honest man. Or who knows, maybe a happy woman, even, kissing a happy man. Who knows? A lustful woman kissing an eager man. I wondered what's happened to him. I don't mean where has he gone, what is he doing. I mean, what happened to him because we kissed." I kept stroking her body. Just as I had the first night when she told me the story of the invasion. Strange that should be, that on two separate nights we lay together like that, the wind coming in the window, Alina telling me about the invasion, me running my hand back and forth along the curve of her body turned first toward me, then away, then toward me again.

Talk about something else. You'll get too full of something—confusion despair unhappiness desire—if you dwell on that night. Too full of memory. Think of Tassiossu of his Madonna. Fantastical figure. The one of Giotto's from the Fourteenth Century. Where the Madonna looks out, with the Christ Child on her knee, with a look on her face of stern, even stoic acceptance of fate. This one, I argued to Tassiossu, was different. It represents a more noble Madonna, a more Greek one in a way, a Madonna ready to acknowledge all tragedy, all death, all sacrifice, even of her then-infant son. He fought me on it. Somewhere, probably from Guillemette I imagine, from Grammatico, Tassiossu put together the elements of an enlarger then blew-up the image he had of the Giotto. He eliminated the angels, the saints surrounding the Madonna and Child. He eliminated their throne. He left only their two faces, along with half of the Madonna's body, down to where her hand holds the Child's knee. See, he argued, the sacrifice of the Child is embedded in a sacrifice by the painter of the Madonna's body, the body of the mother. In offering the Child to fate, she (or he, the painter) offers her own humanity. Only through that offering (by the painter, by the Madonna) can the Christ Child manage to face it. I hung that image on the wall of my office.

People would come into the office startled by that Giotto. Remember the first time that Meleq came in, with Empouche? Meleq laughed. What the hell is that, he said, the new Mother of the Massacred? the Massive Madonna? Our Lady at the End of Days? The Empress of the Emergency Settlement? We drank the cognac that Empouche had with him. That was the first time. Me and Meleq and Empouche. How can there be such pleasures? Beneath Giotto. Who was Giotto? A thousand years. One Thousand. That's all. His optimism, his belief in reality. My own. Even now. I look around me. I belong to this world to no other. Can't help it. Crumbling. Crumbled. The picture now in my mind of Alina kissing that soldier, that poor Government scallywag, sap, killer, bastard. If only Alina were left me. Alina, and that one day with Meleq and Empouche. Or one concert by Lucinda. One evening of her intense un/silence. One sip of the pillaged cognac. I can just about taste it, feel it in my head. The way we talked about the Giotto. The Madonna. The Child. We're not abandoned, we laughed like kids, we've got a bottle of cognac, one cigar for each of us, an afternoon of freedom in which to drink, and The End of War. That's what Empouche called the Settlement because that's what it was for him, The End of War. I could have been executed for letting him stay. An enemy soldier. Any one person who didn't like me could have reported it to the Capital. What chances I was beginning to take. What the hell was I supposed to do, send him back, send him on to invade more villages like Alina's? Had he been in Alina's village? No. I choose to believe that he hadn't. He wasn't. My reality has become the only reality here now. I am no longer the Bureaucrat, I am the Emperor of Reality.

That breeze coming in the window on both those nights. Like it had been ordained.

By whom? By Giotto? What would it be like to sleep with the Madonna? To fuck her? To hold her body. It would be the last. What strange passes you come to. Like sleeping with my wife? Now there's a way to drop yourself into a cauldron of loneliness. Just say it again. My wife. More so than Alina. Some romantic aspect to my brief life with Alina, it doesn't touch the heart of my loneliness. Between us we silently agreed to leave our mutual lonelinesses untouched, to let them survive, even to flourish as we each needed our respective versions of it.

With my wife I had agreed to banish disparate and separate and abominable loneliness from the texture of our lives. I cannot bear to think of the loneliness of her death. There were no suicides. It was worse. I can't. Stop. Don't. Remember the day of drinking under the aegis of the Virgin of the Victorious Vicissitudes in a timeless continuum of companionship the way that Empouche wept that day. Wept he said in happiness at being with two real friends, drinking. Blessed by the Virgin, guarded by the Child. Wept, he said, because he had come to the end not only of war, but of sleep, because he hadn't slept since he arrived in the Settlement, and knew he would never sleep again, so that he wouldn't dream of war. He had become a man whose eyes wouldn't close. Wept, he said, just to be with you, he said to me, and with you, Meleq. The Dante of the Emergency Settlement, he called Meleq. Hugged him and called him that. But I don't write anymore, Meleq said, not until I have exhausted the one *Page* of my book, not until I have turned the secret of resistance within myself to understand it completely, that *Page* with all that is in it, will I write again. Until then I'm a fake, a liar, inauthentic. When I have accepted it I will have earned the right to language again. Empouche was amazed. Hadn't known of Meleq's obsession. Just write! Empouche yelled at Meleq. Do you think that if I tell you the story of my days in the war that I won't be a fake, a liar? Write like your life depends on it and at the same time like it's completely meaningless. The way we're drinking this afternoon. Because this is the last afternoon in the history of the universe. That's how we're drinking today, and if we do it again, Meleq, tomorrow it will be the same way, here under the sign of the Mother of the Moment. Just write, man.

Funny, but now these calmer days are welcome. I even think with calmness right now of those conversations between me and my wife when we had talked of separating.

What Tassiossu said when I asked him what it would mean to him to lie in the lap of the Christian Madonna, to be absorbed by her as he put it, what it would do for him? Would it, I asked him, give him a sense of power? No, he said, it would give him the capacity to accept life as it is. How is it? I asked him. As it is, he said. What is it you can't accept? I asked him. Life, he said, as it is. Oh, yes you can, I argued with him. You do. You accept it completely. You just won't admit it. Do you accept it, he asked me, as it is? What do you mean, I asked him. I mean two or three or four things, he said: one, can you accept history? Can you accept, for example, what has happened to your wife and daughter? Really accept it? Don't you rebel against it, think that it didn't have to happen, that you could have saved them if only this or that or the other thing? Second, yourself, can you accept yourself as you are? Don't you think that someday something will come along to change you, alter you, ascend you, improve you? Third and fourth? I asked him. Third, he said, is me, Tassiossu. Can you accept me as I am? Without hesitation? Without question? Without reservation. Without: oh, I like Tassiossu, I even love Tassiossu, except for his _____ blank? Fill in the blank, he said, think of something you don't like about me then fill it in. Something that separates you from me. Something that prevents you from accepting me in totality. Fourth? I asked him. I can't answer you, he said. I'm working on the fourth. Maybe there will be none. Maybe the fourth has to do with accepting it all with joy. Oh, Tassiossu, I'll tell you the fourth right now. To accept —I'll put this in the most concrete terms I can imagine. I'll boil it down to one thing which will represent the whole thing. Can I accept a world without you, Tassiossu? After the way our conversations began with such hesitation, with lies, deceptions (I must have had my own with you as well), then became theoretical, ideas, then became personal, feelings, commitments. Can I accept a world in which you are no longer here pursuing the hidden tones in the image of the Christian Madonna? Your pursuit was urgent and endless. You were right. Its urgency is felt in the intensity of its absence. If only you had succeeded instead of dying. I used to think, for a time, that in your death you achieved what you were after, that your body gave itself in, all its grief, all its resistance, all its non-acceptance, completely to the Great Mother, to Mother Earth, to Mother Life. You literally ex/pired, out-breathed into the lap of the Madonna. Now I castigate myself, I tell myself that's my own romantic hallucination. You could only achieve it alive. Only. Not dead, not dying. Now I'm here alone, Tassiossu. I people this paper with you, with Lucinda, with Meleq, Rivka, with Abanno, with everyone. We all survived through those last tribulations didn't we? And then...? And I'm writing it down so that we can read it, the we I suppose who is me. Read it as I'm writing it. Don't worry, old pal, dear Tassiossu of the Mutatious Madonna, it is not done yet.

Deeper. Deeper than ever. Not deeper. Different. How different? More solitary? No, less alone, really. Figures of the imagination, no, of the memory. Really? Not different. Finally. No, not finally, continually. Not different, the same. Not the same.

Do you remember, Tassiossu (ah! I have a reader! even if he won't ever read this, at least as I write it I have a reader), how Abanno and I tried to organize the water project? Fantastical Abanno. All the macchine of the Gruppo delle Macchine Festive he had stripped down to their bare bones: wheels pulleys pedals. Then used them to transport water from the boiling pots—the Holy Water Purification Pits you called them— back into the Settlement, to the people, the lines of people. After we discovered that we couldn't trust the water from the Government pipelines anymore. Then from the Government trucks. Good God I remember that. Those people so sick, dying of it. Oh Tassiossu you called it the Impure Waters from the Corrupted Source. But Abanno, I mean, Abanno, I wanted to talk about, because I so admired him in those days. An entire industry. A refinery but of water, not oil. Of the primary, not the luxurious. The projects he organized. The people he put to work. The food alone for the workers at the boiling pits. Those pots, Tassiossu, do you remember those pots? They're still there. Grammatico is a stubborn fool, he wouldn't be put off he kept going building those things.

All right. I give it up. There is no Tassiossu to be talking to. I write to no one. But I go on. I accept the world as it is, Tassiossu. He was manipulative, Abanno, yes, but he got it done. People drank water and didn't die, they drank it and didn't get sick, they drank it and lived. Abannowater they called it. That parade we had for him. Well, they had for him. They asked for it, it wasn't my idea initially. Carrying him down the street, through the ruins of ancient buildings, throwing buckets of water over him. The song they wrote: Abannowater. That rough sign out by the purification pits: Survival City Water Works. All those fires going day and night. I am of two minds right now. Part of me moans: but we had such life in us! against such odds! In the midst of such circumstance! We had Abannogenius. How could it all be put to waste? How could it! While the other part of me looks backs to remember, then feels: yes, we had such life in us! In the midst of such circumstances! I am fulfilled. Isn't that odd. Do I even believe it? I can hardly believe it. That I feel that way. That I feel both those ways. That I want to go on writing it. I, who saw it all with my own eyes, I can hardly believe it.

Do you remember Lucinda's concert out by the Water Works? Oh, remember on the walk on the way out there, to her concert. That's when I saw the guy who sat on the edge of that building—how I had thought of restoring some of these buildings; enlisting architects, engineers, estimating dangers of collapse, requirements for shoring up here or there to save some pillar, column, wall, abutment. Let them collapse. Let them all collapse? The collapse of an entire world, all its foundations. Ruin as inevitable destination and all my efforts my palliations as counter-visionary, blind, just frightened attempts to hold up what had already fallen. What if now at this very moment I finally accepted all the ruin, decay, dissolution, ruination, what would follow? What have they done to tear this world to shreds, how they have taken it in their claws, their teeth, and torn it, slashed it, bled it, dismembered it. Could I stand here in the midst of it? Could I even stand here and accept it, as Tassiossu talked about acceptance? Or even his fourth element?

Well, I was walking along—did the most ancient narratives have digressions like mine? Did the Greek reciters sit back once in a while and talk about what was on their minds? Did the tribal narrators? I was walking to the Water Works for the concert Lucinda would do there for the workers.

It was certainly one of Lucinda's greatest. Oh yes. Her discipline, her attention, her precision. She knew she was in the midst of something. Her silence. Her violin on her lap. Unturned throughout. The loud pounding of the fires burning, forty-six of them. The sun. The hills there on the other side of the fire pits. Watching all those people, maybe two hundred of them gathered around her, standing by their cauldrons, by their work stations, on the road, listening. I heard the violin then. Absolutely. Not just as wind-harp. I heard the music it made. Most clearly that day. That's when I first knew that it had to be an excellent violin, I would not have heard that had it not been. No, it had to be what it was, what Lucinda had carried here with her. An unwavering tone. To produce that sound. In the body of the violin. Abanno standing there. Just now I think of the sound of that violin, of the way it affected Abanno, the way you could see it the way his body absorbed the sound of the violin and the sounds around him, and the way that soldier's voice entered Alina's body, the way it was there somewhere in her body in her blood yet I was unable to retrieve it. Lucinda's concert that day reduced all life to sound, collecting life into that one…what? space of hearing, music of the spheres but here, right here, fires burning, people shuffling, coughs, wind, carts set still yet creaking, the music from the violin, inherent in it, issued from it. Had Abanno been able to finish his water project. What a triumph that would have been! To have had water flowing. Down from the mountains. Into our desert. It's a simple thing, he kept saying. It's just mechanics, but it takes time. There's no mystery to it, like to Lucinda's concerts, it just takes time. Like a child I ask, how could it all have failed? How could there not have been enough time?

God I feel sick, suddenly. Must stop writing. No strength left for it now. Nausea.

Begin again today with a real lingering bitterness, where does this bitterness come from which rose up in me yesterday won't recede? Or better perhaps ask how I've staved it off so long. One more thing to accept. If I'm to get to the end. Of what? A narrative? There is none. A writing? And then what? Well, then be free to work on other things, yes? On what? On the waterworks? What if I were to finish the damn thing all by myself, what if I were to stand here alone over the completed project? Then what? A strange course your questions are taking. Yesterday after resting for a while I went out to walk around the Settlement. (To whom are you talking?

To the same as always.) Even though there will be no way to get photographs developed, I took my camera because I wanted to see things that way again, through the lens of a camera. Without film. The camera, the act of looking, not the film, inscribes memory. On the plaza, looking through the lens finder, I saw the Gruppo delle Macchine Imaginarie all over again, heard their music, saw the crowd. Saw the bright greens, reds, yellows of their paper-and-wire insects, their flowering garden of wood. As I looked it all dissolved. It became quiet. My own breath came through my nose, my eye up against the camera's eye. Turned the camera. Saw the old slat-wooded benches around the plaza. Photographed them. Clicked the shutter. Click. Turned to the ruins of the church on the north end. Where the colonnade had been. Even had been still standing during the performance of the Gruppo. Photographed my imagination of the old colonnade. What a great thing is a colonnade: how it encloses a space which by that very enclosure is opened wide. Contradiction is the root core of perception? Then photographed the ruins of the colonnade, of the stone church. Turned back then to the bench where I'd seen the drunk young couple after the Gruppo's performance. Saw them there for a moment's flash, but didn't click the camera. Then their absence appeared, then I took the photograph, just of the bench. Something happened, something turned in me yesterday, I don't know what it was. As though, in the midst of the Emergency Settlement at the end of its existence with no one left I entered an Emergency of my own. The nausea. And that bitterness. Well, they're related aren't they? Then today out with a filmless camera taking photographs of things that don't exist of things that do. As though I have come to a certain pleasure of the emptiness, of the absence.

Was the old divine creature itself God in ruin and so created a universe, out of ruin? As would I? A universe of circus performers of drunken lovers of waterworks projects of friends dining drinking talking of music and theories and ideas?

Grab on to something you're slipping. Not good for you. Grab on to what? The young couple I saw on the first day here? Some bulwark against too much. Fine. The young couple you saw on the first day here. You were out walking, you were trying to get a feel for the place you were trying to understand it. It was before Alina. It was perhaps before your wife and daughter were killed. You can't know. You think they weren't dead yet. You walked out looking for something else besides just knowledge of the place, didn't you? You walked out looking for some answer to some question you couldn't even pose to yourself. What was it? Can you imagine it now? No. I still can't. All right. Go on, then. You walked out you saw a great deal. You saw how every building, once its structure had been attacked by disuse or bombs, had come down by the force of gravity. You saw the inner structure of buildings laid bare and you found it compelling, you found in it a certain fascination. It was something to work with, you imagined. It was a lay of a land. You saw a lot of people, strangers who were now under your jurisdiction whatever that might mean. Under your care. You were responsible. You liked that. You were up to it. You kept walking, accepting your responsibility even amidst your incredible fact of Emergency. It set you going. Then you came up a small side street on the way back to the Bureau and that's when you saw them first. They weren't touching, they sat quietly drinking from those paper cups. It was a cool afternoon so you imagined the coffee or the chocolate or the tea or the soup was hot, was warming them. They didn't see you. You were responsible for them. You thought to yourself, I am not of them, but I am responsible for them. I, who am not of anyone now. It was a strange sensation to feel, suddenly aware of it, a deep isolation, aloneness. Bleak, yes, but thereby determined. Bleak, suddenly, yes, but not defeated. (Even now, how is it possible, not defeated.) Do I imagine this now only because I'm here, writing to no one, so have become dislocated, strange? No, it is true. I felt oddly isolated, still feel it, even though there is now no one to be isolated from. At the time I thought that I suffered from an isolation I would be cured of. How? By administering to the Emergency Settlement? I know, you're feeling a particular anxiety now about all this, but go on. Stick with reality. The couple. Well, there they were. I watched them with enormous pleasure, more pleasure maybe than I've ever had as a participant in such a couple. No, that's not true is it? Is it? I can't tell. I watched them as the boy moved from facing the girl to her side. Then put his arm around her, she turned, put her arms around him, they embraced, they pulled back to face each other, they kissed, they moved in closer to each other. Why did you find out their names, have their records pulled, why did you read their dossiers in your office? I don't know. Why do I feel like you're interrogating me now? Like I'm interrogating me? I did nothing wrong. What if I saw them as a symbol of something? Nothing is a symbol of anything else. Everything is a thing unto itself everyone a thing unto himself, herself. Talk about reconstructing life…if I could resurrect those two right now it would be enough to begin with, wouldn't it.

Like mine with Alina had never become. It had become exhausted, but then renewed. We had quarreled. We had been alienated from one another. But we found each other again. I don't think we had ever devolved into the desperation I had seen in those two in the plaza. Nihilistic. They wanted to destroy each other in order to be created anew, incorrupt. I don't think I ever knew that kind of nihilism, yet it, too, fascinated me. It must have, and that's why it's stuck with me. That's why it's threatened the innocence perhaps or the hope of the young couple I saw. What was their nihilism their urge to destroy each other? Nothing like the destruction of the Pageant of the Macchine. Is it akin to the painful urge I have had since this morning, since yesterday, to create the world? A world. LucindaAlinaAbanno all of them all of it. Certainly there were times—some of them making love with Alina, with my wife,— when I would feel full of a fury or a rage or a powerful force. But never an urge to nihilism like that. They could have literally disappeared into each other as they actually did disappear this morning before my camera, although in that case they disappeared into reality, they disappeared, reality appeared. An empty bench. Not so much a reality as a presence, yet a presence embedded with something in the fact of it. What is that something? That one night with Alina when she told me of the invasion as I followed her body over and over and over with my hand, that night I think may have been the one time when I felt most the fullness of the world, the actuality of it. Even though part of it was a lie, it was no less full. I don't care about the lie, of course, why would I care? Everyone has their reasons for lying; Alina's that night are easy enough to understand. How could she admit to me that night that she had embraced that young soldier, kissed him, held him to her? She and Tassiossu both lied to me out of a sense of self-preservation. Tassiossu feared my administrative power; Alina feared the judgment of her lover against her, maybe her own judgment against herself. Why would I judge her? Didn't I understand perfectly why she embraced that soldier? Didn't I know that it was in fact the absolute opposite of nihilism? Who was he? Our soldier? Their soldier? Who cares? Didn't I imagine the two of them, Alina and the soldier, in that embrace as a kind of primeval couple? Wasn't I, anyway, by the time of that night in my bedroom with Alina, wasn't I already beyond judgment? Nearly. There were those against whom judgment was the only way to stay alive: my superior in the Capital, those in power. A few of them. Maybe it was the fact that I had come, by living in the Emergency Settlement, by seeing so much, by understanding the moral quandary of a principle like self-preservation, that I had come to judge almost no one, isn't it because of that that I was able, that night with Alina, to feel as I did, the fullness of the world, even in my body, in my hands, in my eyes. Calm defeated fullness. That breeze. Her one lie in her many truths. I saw them—Alina and the soldier—as a primeval couple not because of the union of his violence with the passion of her suffering. Because of the inexplicable impulse of it. Impulse revealed in inexplicability. A moment of uncontingent necessity. Later, when Alina asked me to explain it to her, how I saw it, what I thought it meant, I had to tell her that I didn't know what it meant. It had no meaning in the usual sense of those words. Embracing the enemy, betrayal born of desire, the powerless seeking the power of the powerful, of trying to reach with the tongue of her kiss into the cortex of the violence physically to dissipate it, physically to diffuse it. I saw it, I told her, as something which is. As action. Even once, when we were talking about it, having coffee together in AJ's, I told her that I saw it as universal action.

That was the day we began the ritual of massage. Shall I write it? Why not? Yes, for the personal pleasure of the memory of it. In the sense that writing is a kind of living. That saying something, no, specifically writing something, gives it life now. I still believe instinctually if not rationally in that kind of power of writing. Archaic power. Like the cave paintings we found near here. Yes yes yes. Do you remember that? Meleq and Rivka and I were out walking beyond the Settlement, into the foothills where we found a cave we wandered into very warily. It was immediately cool. As we descended, yet cooler. Fantastic place. The Original Cave we called it. We came back, got flashlights, water, then we got Tassiossu, thinking he might know something historically, which he did, of course. He's the one who found the handprint, and I'm sure it's because he was so alert to the distinction of it as art. He was convinced it was prehistoric, but how could we know without tests. Did it matter if it were prehistoric or made yesterday, I argued, the impulse behind it was the same. Tassiossu argued that its hue, that its shape suggested the primitive method of taking paint into the mouth in the form of vegetable dyes, putting the hand against the wall, then spitting over the hand to leave a positive impression of negative space. As Rivka remembered, she had done as a child in school. She agreed with me: it didn't matter whether it had been done prehistorically or yesterday. Tassiossu insisted that for him it gained resonance if done prehistorically, it gained a depth of echo, it reflected such an ancient, pre-ancient pre-literate human quality, urge, need, impulse. It stunned him, Tassiossu said. Days after we'd first seen it, Tassiossu considered it alongside his collection of the Madonna. I forced him to work this material up into a public lecture, which he did, prefaced by a small performance by the Gruppo, a piece they did in masks. Shall I describe that? It was terrific. No. I'll let it go. For now. I'll come back to it. I think people understood Tassiossu more the more they heard him. He said that the Original Cave hand print related to the Madonna image in several ways: since we don't know how early the hand print is, we don't know its relationship to the development of language. Let's say, Tassiossu speculated, that the image was made before language had reached a complex level; it consisted perhaps of a few monosyllabic utterances. The hand print in that case represents a great leap forward in that—as visual language—it is far in advance of word-based language: it communicates on many levels: it presents a concrete image of the desire to create artistically; it leaves a mark indicating that the maker wants to be known by others who see it, or by imagined others (gods?) who might see it; it marks space, changing it: the region in the cave where the hand print is made becomes an art gallery, a specialized region in which the hand print performs the linguistic function of announcing certain information to others; others read it: seeing it, in the absence of the one who made it, they have certain reactions to it in their own minds; it is abstract, as is all painting: it isn't a hand, it isn't the representation of a hand; it isn't even the absence of the hand: it is an abstraction given shape by the body of the artist. It gives coherence, presence, identity to a people. It continues, Tassiossu said, to do so. We, in the Emergency Settlement, are as much a part of that prehistoric community as were the people who lived in the Original Cave, as was the person who made the hand painting.

There were several other digressions in Tassiossu's lecture. He speculated on its meaning were it made at various other times in the history of language. Then he drew comparisons to the images of the Madonna, all of which he said were visual languages of an order more sophisticated—not better, only more codified—than the hand. He ran through three or four Madonna paintings, explaining all their symbols, then asked the audience: were they moved more by the Madonna paintings or by the hand painting.

Almost everyone said they were more moved by the hand painting. Everyone had seen it. We had our own tourist site set up. People left personal objects nearby, tributes, small things whose significance often was known only to the person who left it. In addition we'd cut a piece of rock from near the hand painting on which to make a replica. Tassiossu and Rivka did it, experimenting with colors and dyes for days, then reconstructing it by using the hand-and-spitting method by which they thought it had been originally made. So Tassiossu had a concrete sample to show that evening. He also showed slides of the four Madonna paintings he discussed that night—on a projection system Grammatico designed and built using wax to create the light. (Where did he get the wax?) I remember my favorite of those slides that night was a Lorenzetti. It stung me, really, because I remember the Child looking so frightened, helpless, the Madonna in this case utterly serene, not anguished at all, placid, content, full of the knowledge of the turbulence ahead for her Child, even the extreme suffering, yet so calm she was not human. She held the Child with very human hands, the slight muscular strain in them. The Child's left arm reached around his mother's neck, then behind her held the soft cloth of her hooded cape, holding on to whatever he could find while at the same time pulling himself up against the Madonna, helping her to support him. It was a desperate look in his face: he, too, knew, but had a very different response to his fate than did the Madonna. The whole was backgrounded by one of those ornate medieval golden boards in the shape of a church window. I have a sketch of it here in this very notebook somewhere if I can find it. In her serenity, I argued later with Tassiossu, this Lorenzetti Madonna does carry an aspect of Kali as she embodies a very sweet divine indifference, an absolute unresisted acceptance. Kali, in her creative or her preservative or her destructive phase, Tassiossu argued back, is anything but indifferent. In each phase, she embodies the passion of that phase. Strangely enough, that night of Tassiossu's lecture, Lucinda, whom I thought for sure would vote a preference for the hand painting, said she was more moved by the Madonna figures. For her, the hand painting was an indecipherable image, created in a culture so far removed in time it was difficult for her to appreciate the layers of meaning it may contain. She said this publicly, during a question period. Tassiossu was enamored with her comment. I agree with you, Tassiossu said, that everything I have said about the meaning of the hand painting is speculation based on my knowledge of art, of art theory, of my own personal understanding of art, of symbols, of meaning itself. I suspect that my speculations are accurate. What you add is a dimension of unknowning, of a limitless possibility of knowing we will never penetrate and so becomes an impossibility of knowing which hovers around or in the image of the hand painting like the missing lines of some ancient fragmentary poem. That makes the hand painting, Tassiossu continued, resonate with the unknown that we sometimes call the mysterious but which is our actual human condition. Yes, Lucinda agreed. But, Tassiossu went on, that realm of unknowing is much like what we encounter in your concerts, so I'd think you would be more drawn to the hand painting. It's more akin to your own work.

Everyone had a laugh. I don't like to talk about my concerts, Lucinda responded, but I will say that everything in my concerts is known, my concerts are of the known, even though it may be a different knowing at each concert, but also, if—a very big if, she said—if there is an aspect of unknowing to my concerts, then it's enough unknowing for me and I prefer the Madonna images where I feel connected with the known. Again, everyone had a laugh because, of course, we all feel a huge unknowing in Lucinda's concerts. But perhaps we are wrong. Perhaps she is right perhaps what we feel is a huge knowing.

Where is the replica of the hand painting we made for that evening's lecture? I'd like to copy it into this book. For the first time it makes me think that what I'm making is a book. An object. How could the handpainting artist of the Original Cave have known who would stumble onto their work? They couldn't. Do I hope that by making this into a book, wherein I copy things like handpaintings, italic lettering, sketches of Madonnas as well as diagrams of waterworks that it will have a reader, readers? We put that replica of the hand painting in the office where the enlargement of the Giotto Madonna still hangs.

I'll walk out there. It's not that far. I want to see the Original Hand again. Maybe I'll walk out as far as the waterworks. I've been afraid to go out there. Thought the sorry sight of it would kill me, but it's all right. It's time, I think, to do that kind of thing. To go where I'd been afraid of going. Although walking back that far into the cave by myself could be not so wise. No, I'll go. It's alright. Where was Alina that day we first went out there? She wasn't with us. Wasn't that the day she met with her group? No, of course not, that was the day she went out hiking alone. Yes. When she said that something was happening to her she could understand only by being out alone for a long time. Yes. It was that day because it was that night that she didn't come back at all. Yes. Rivka kept asking me about her that afternoon while we were walking said she had a disturbing dream about Alina though Meleq kept trying to reassure her saying that disturbing dreams about other people never come true, they represent something going on in yourself, but Rivka was sure it was actually about Alina. Remember? Rivka was frantic later that night when she couldn't find Alina, while Meleq and Tassiossu and even I were so involved in the excitement of the painted hand discovery and I thought anyway that Alina was fine. How could I be so blind at times? So in the dark? So unaware not of myself but of someone as close to me as Alina? What if she hadn't resolved her despair out there, wherever she was, what if she had ended her life just then, jumped off some cliff. Tassiossu said we should look for her. Maybe I was more aware than I give myself credit for. Maybe what I thought, that we had to leave her alone, was the best thing. But come on, admit it, it wasn't because you knew what was going on with her just then. It was just the way you reacted. Genuinely. Selfishly?

Maybe too selfishly that time.

And it was Empouche who found Alina. Not that she needed to be found. She had run her round. She apologized to me. I'm sorry, she said, I didn't mean to worry you. I went off to die. Something of what holds me up, she said, collapsed. I can describe it literally, she said, physically. Something snapped, something which had always pulled me up, away from, out of hopelessness. It couldn't pull me up and out of it. I sank into a gloom where I saw it was neverending. Even my love for you, she said, partakes of that perpetual gloom, can't be separated from it because we know where we are, we know where we're going. How can we throw ourselves into each other's arms promising each other anything? We're balm for each other now on a laceration that won't heal. We are happiness for each other with a happiness that grows out of a void. That's all right, she said. I'm not asking for anything more. I'm not accusing you of any insufficiency. I just couldn't pull myself up out of that obscure gloom. I went into the canyons and the desert. I was sure I would just let myself fall over a cliffside and that would be it. Why not? I would sit on top of one of the cliffs, lean out, fall. Who really needs me now? You do? The people from my village do? Yes. That made it very difficult. That may have been the beginning of what prevented me. I struggled against it. I tried to reduce you and them to the gloom. You can reduce yourself to that, but not others. So instead of dropping over the clifftop I sat up there. I couldn't dispel the feeling, the weight of it in my stomach. I stayed there waiting for some opening in the fog, some light to come through. That didn't happen. I only saw through all that fog that I could endure it, live within it. It was merely a question of whether I absorbed the fog or the fog absorbed me. I tried to convince myself that I could make something out of it, make use of it, but what could I make of it? It's the condition of these days. Who am I to create icons of it? Better, I thought, to just let it be. I wondered, could I even get up to walk with it, the weight of it physically seemed to be that stupefying. I stood up there rather slowly. I found that I could walk. I'm so silly, she said. If I could just have a vision, I kept thinking, if I could just see some other world, or see this world in some other way. If I could turn what has happened into something. I stayed the whole night because I thought that by my tenacity I could force some revelation. It was a long night. Cold at times, but I could walk to warm myself up for a while. This, I finally accepted it, would be the vision that I would have: that I have imbibed this Emergency of ours, assimilated, absorbed, accepted it, and that's all that I could ask for. So I'm back. I came back. Empouche found me asleep beyond the perimeter because on the way back I was so exhausted I just fell asleep.

I offered to massage Alina that night. I thought at the time, I remember I thought it was somehow ironic, the juxtaposition of our discovery of the hand painting in the Original Cave and Alina's absent vigil. We had already begun our ritual of massaging each other. But she insisted that she massage me that night. We had been talking outside late that afternoon, sitting on the edge of a ruined wall, drinking sips of Empouche's liberated cognac. She took me back to my apartment, told me to take off my clothes while she prepared the bed for massage. I sat for quite a while in my robe waiting for her. I sat in the living room, she busied herself in the bedroom. I saw her there. Once or twice she looked back to see me. When everything was ready, she called me in. She had changed into a robe. The bed was fresh. The room was cleaned up. I protested again. I should be massaging you tonight, Alina. You're the one who's been through so much. But she insisted. No, she said, maybe I'm the one now who has the strength to massage you. More slowly, more deliberately than usual, she began to massage my head. She took a long time, rubbing my scalp, the small muscles around my eyes, my cheeks, my jaws. As she moved down my body reactions surprised me, unfolding. I concentrated just on the act of Alina's hands. Just the act of it. I went through a hundred stages of reaction: I was suspicious: why is she doing this; I was resentful: why has she taken my prerogative from me, taken over; I was desirous: touch my body everywhere, take it into your hands; I felt lust yet I made no move; I felt a tenderness itself made up of a hundred strands of compassion, pity, respect, openness, sorrow, regret, union and communion; images went through my mind: armies clashing, friends' faces, my daughter in her last fearsome moment to which I had abandoned her, until all that was left either of vision or emotion was the sensation of what I felt from Alina's hands: the reverse of what I felt of her in my hands the night we lay in bed while she told me of the invasion of her village. She wanted me to give her my body without reservation. That she could do what she wanted with it entirely. What she wanted was not so much to message it as to be in the act of messaging it. The act of relaxing my body as an activity to stave off everything: first, as action, and second, almost as if in some sort of trance of messaging, an act of urgency, the way she had kissed the soldier on the porch of her family's house during the invasion. As though this cleansing could be an act of pure urgency beyond meditation or repentance or apology or love. I lost the perception of my own body as I became aware of how absorbed Alina had become in the act of massage. She was trying to obliterate both of our bodies to bring us together into a state of nonbeing. As she did so, being kept asserting itself in one form or another, in some thought, in some bodily pain. We approached this state of nonbeing she strove for. My passivity/her action each nullifying the other. The focus of her action/the progressive degree of my yielding combining to form the possibility of a creative nihilism through which we sensationalized being, to which we were encouraged approach by the constant reminder even of the very air around us. As Alina massaged my body, at that dissolution/communion's approach, we would enter it briefly, then it would recede. Alina would renew her efforts on my skin. Her bitterness, exhausting itself, became tenderness. The tenderness became lightness. Finally, we slept.

The next day Empouche came to the office to check up on Alina, to tell me what had happened. I was busy when he arrived, meeting with a group of citizens who wanted to talk to me about supporting certain religious activities. I went out to meet Empouche, though. He told me how bad Alina had been when he'd found her. Dehydrated, weak. She made him take her to his house for a few hours to recover so I wouldn't see her so diminished. She was concerned that I had enough to worry about without adding herself as a burden. I asked Empouche what he'd been doing out there. He said he'd gone for a long hike to think things over, that lately he'd been haunted by things he'd done as a soldier. What could I say? I looked at him perhaps for too long without saying anything, imagining what he might have done, how he might feel, trying to think of what to say. Thank you, I finally said, for bringing Alina back. I told him we should all cook dinner together soon, with a few others, whom should we invite? I feel so strange. What was I doing? As though I was back with my wife and my daughter planning some dinner party for our friends. Well, I was with Alina and Empouche and Meleq and Paolo and all the others and what else were we doing? We might certainly as well plan some dinner parties.

Which led actually to the dinner party we had with Empouche and Lucinda and Paolo and Abanno and Grammatico and Klaus and Hwang, Meleq having been sick that night. But why talk about that? Why write it? Now? When there are other, more important things to write. How importance becomes relative. How sitting out here in the sunshine working at this desk I imagine I could look up to find myself in some cafe having a drink, writing reports on this or that to the higher-ups. *Report on the Condition of Crops in the Emergency Settlement in the Western Quadrant*; *Report on*

MARTIN NAKELL

*the Establishment of Schools in the Emergency Settlement in the
Western Quadrant; Report on the Meeting of the Citizens' Council
of the Emergency Settlement in the Western Quadrant; Report
on the Issuance of Currency in the Emergency Settlement in the
Western Quadrant; Report on the Importance of Regulated Water
Supply to the Emergency Settlement in the Western Quadrant;
Report on the Sighting of Troop Movements from the Emergency
Settlement in the Western Quadrant.* Some things, of course,
I never reported on because I finally knew better. Finally, I
understood the true nature of life in the Capital. Yet, how I
hadn't seen it earlier, how I had gone on believing there were
people above me all the way to the top who had some interest
in the welfare of our citizens. How was it I came to see it finally
to accept it? After my meeting with the President? During my
meeting with the President? No, during that meeting I was
just shocked, I think, to discover a man so petty, so rigid, so
obviously out of touch with ordinary reality and so out of
touch with himself, a man so given to the sentimentality of
cliché and so distant from the substance of life. How warmly
he welcomed me into his office, how he lauded what he called
the magnitude of my work, the sanctity of the Settlement itself
where people suffering the most dire consequences of war's
displacement could find refuge with security in a safe haven.
How he described it as a kind of commune where we could
all learn from each other, grow as human beings, be tested by
the exigencies of the Emergency to become the best each one
could become, how we could foster love and brotherhood in
an atmosphere protected from the unfortunate but righteous

war, how he encouraged us to set up programs to develop the highest quality of each resident, even those from the most foreign of cultures. Had he no clue what was happening? What he himself had done to bring us to this state? Was I more shocked at his perilous innocence or the quickness of my own anger, how it came charging out of me despite the risk. I had gone to the Capital after all to talk about real things, problems, to petition for help. I had gone with the concurrence of everyone around me in the Settlement. Christ! Even Grammatico even Guillemette were in on those discussions I mean I wasn't the only complete idiot to believe we could have an influence in the Capital. Were my wife and my daughter killed because of the way I insisted to the President? No damnit. They were already dead by that time and the bastard must have known it. I know he knew it.

On the way out of his office, after we had calmed down, I passed through an outer office, a waiting room. An official whom I recognized, someone I had met during my years in the Government, leaned back on a couch with documents in hand, going over them. Like so many in those days, he looked exhausted. He was nearly reclined on the couch. Having not yet closed the outer door, I heard as the President came into the waiting room screaming at that poor guy on the couch. I opened the door a crack to see the scene: Take your goddamn feet off that couch or I'll have your fucking head do you hear me I'll have it in a minute I won't even think about it who the fuck do you think you are putting your dirty feet up on the furniture around here do you think this is a campground in some muddy field of battle you'd better learn how to behave or your life isn't worth a grain of the salt that I see is delivered to your cozy apartment each week with your privileged grocery lists do you hear me! Do you hear me? I've had enough of you and your filthy crap! Get off! get your feet off of that couch! Fucking barbarian!

On the train ride back to the Settlement I was sure that man was killed on the spot, shot, that instant. Then I knew how far we had fallen. Then I knew the fate of my wife and my daughter. Then I feared completely for the Emergency Settlement. Then I called that meeting when I got back. Then I knew it was up to me and I, careening into the knowledge that it wasn't at all up to me, who was too small for the job, but all of us any of us everyone. Our survival was unlikely. I only wanted not to lose Alina, the one person whom I knew from the very beginning I would have to lose. The way she came into my office that first day I knew when I looked at her that she had already given up everything herself so that whatever she did now was contingent upon certain events in the past which for her erased all actual possibility. The way she spoke to me that first day, asking for extraordinary medical supplies for the people from her village, I knew she was trying to save the remnants of people she already considered to be ghosts and I knew that I wouldn't accept that view of our situation that I was determined to revivify those ghosts to make a life of it. That was before my meeting with the President. After my meeting with him the first person I saw when I got back was Alina. How was I going to tell her: Yes, Alina, you were right from the very first day. You had seen things I hadn't yet seen, but now I've seen them first hand. I couldn't tell her that because she would then be the one to comfort me, while I wanted at that moment to protect her. What did I say, I said something like: It went badly. She shook her head. We drove from the train station to the restaurant where Ynorob had dinner waiting for us.

Ynorob's dinners. That he was preparing food for us only out of what he had, that he's no longer anywhere doing that. How can it be that in those days even in those circumstances he made those extraordinary meals for us that lightened our minds, literally. Your mind itself which, incorporeal as it seems to be, yet can be physically heavy.

What if someone found this writing someday? What if they wandered into the Settlement long after I was gone, rummaged around, came into the office, opened my desk, found a stack of papers, a notebook, rifled through them, took them outside to sit on the edge of a ruin, began to read. Read about the fact that no one would ever read this. They might think to themselves that it's true, that no one ever reads anything, that all that goes into writing is never read by a reader, it's what escapes language, that all writing is the skeleton only the remnants. Or they might think that, alas, maybe I hoped no one would ever read it, maybe I sought the obscurity not for myself but for my work because only in obscurity would it last forever, would it coincide with the eternal. Or, they might join my hope that it might be found, be read, rescued, distributed to those few who might be interested. Then Alina would have life again. Lucinda would. Abanno. Ibrahim. The person who finds it might start one of those controversies about found manuscripts. Everyone would believe that they hadn't really found it, but had written it, and to gain a readership had given it an air of the exotic by declaring they had found it. What if they had even put in these last two sentences to seal its authenticity, even this sentence? Yes. Find it. Yes. Save it. Publish. Distribute. Read. Discuss it. Even among your friends, your colleagues. Let it begin to take hold, even slowly.

OK, if not for my sake alone, for Alina's. All right. I got lost for a time. Neither for my sake nor for Alina's. Let it disappear then. Let nothing remain of her memory. Because I feared him, she said. I close my eyes to imagine her fear. What fear, at that moment? Destruction? Alina's fear that the Ninth Soldier would destroy her? She kissed him to defer her own destruction? To incorporate it? I asked her, Did you close your eyes when you kissed him? She said, Yes. Did you fear he would become part of you? I asked her. Yes, she said. Now I close my eyes to see what she saw. Not so much the soldier, or the kiss even, but the fear she felt become a part of her. Why? So she might control it? No, I see it now, with my eyes closed: so she might be ready for it, so that destruction from without would meet embrace from within, so that it would not be foreign, so that it would be acceptable. Is that something I have to learn from her? She told me that later, as the kiss with that soldier became part of our ongoing our seamless conversation, broken only by brief absences from each other of a few hours, or a day, or, when she went off to commit suicide, more than a day. But except for her suicide journey, when I lost contact with her, our conversations were a continuous outgrowth of one seed. Even now the seed is not inert. In an Emergency Settlement, with nothing to hang on to, with everything around you going to ruin, with each project of hope a clear act of desperation, then to have this continuous outgrowth of words. That the word is the tip of the iceberg, born of the body not just the mind, that it is conceived in the heat of the sun and the shit of the earth like a fruit a vegetable an herb that it tastes of its origins. Understanding that the word is an object woven of time in space. And vice versa. Is that why I write? To keep the word alive to keep Alina alive thereby others thereby myself? Perhaps. So part of the dialogue between me and Alina included an ongoing discourse on the kiss. At another time she told me that she had kissed the soldier not out of fear but out of pure lust. Pure lust? I pushed her on it. Yes, she said, she had been excited, aroused, lustful. The chaos of that military force invading her village. But they were there to annihilate you! I protested. I'm just telling you, she said, what happened. That I was aroused. That I wanted to feel the flesh of his mouth against mine, his face against mine, his body. He wore so much military gear I hardly did feel his body, though I did feel his mouth and his tongue and his face and his breath. Stop! I yelled at her. Are you jealous? she asked me. Yes, I said, I'm jealous. How can you talk about your passion for some dolt of a soldier, someone whose whole sense of power comes only from joining in with a hierarchy of murder, someone who represents everything I struggle against, and not expect me to be outraged by it, jealous, rejected. I'm sorry, she apologized. Of course I can see you would feel that way. It's not what I intended. She rolled onto me—we lay in bed again when she told me that—her head came into my shoulder, she glared out the window. For a few minutes I sulked. Then, I'm sorry, I said. I'm not sorry I felt jealous; I'm sorry I questioned the lust you felt for the soldier. I don't question it I understand it. What a dance we did on what a high wire.

You shouldn't feel jealous, she said, you know we can't promise each other too much now.

Was what I did then foolish? I will never know. It was and it wasn't, the eternal bipolarity of existence: it is and it isn't. So I was foolish and wise in the same breath. I said, tell me, then, about the lust. And she did, telling me about his clumsy uniform, the artifacts of war strapped to his waist, his chest, his helmet. Yet, how they succeeded, the two of them, in a moment of lust between them, a lust aroused in both of them by the war around them, the sense of ruin even more than the sense of destruction. How ruin reveals lust, engenders it, enlists it, revels in it, or vice versa, how lust revels in ruin. Yes, I said, that is part of what happens to us here, in the Settlement, isn't it? Yes, Alina said, it is. For a moment with that soldier it was an explosion of it; with us, she said, it is a continuum, like our discourse. Less noticeable, more significant. Whatever is more significant is so often less noticeable, must be seen to be seen.

We talked to Meleq about all this once. It got mentioned in his presence, so Alina told him about it. She didn't reveal her reasons for kissing the soldier to Meleq. She only told him that it had happened. He was furious with her. How could you do that! he accused her. Back off, I said to him. You don't understand her. I understand, he said, that while her family was being herded out of their home by a squad of punks and hoodlums she stopped to bestow her favors on one of them. Then Alina offered him an explanation. She leaned over (we were sitting in a café), put her hand on his, and said to him: Meleq, trust me a little. The reason I did it was to save my family. Do you see? And it may have been what kept us alive. Maybe I distracted that soldier just long enough, who knows? But we all lived. I'm sorry, Meleq apologized. How could I have accused you. Only because those roving bands of sanctified gangsters have done the same thing to all of us, only because the whole situation has us all on edge. I apologize, Meleq repeated.

Later, I congratulated Alina. On her quick thinking, on her poise, on saving what could have been a bad divide between us. But she told the truth, she said. That kiss had been an act of sabotage. I approached her as gently as I could. How, I asked her, can I accept that, when you have told me that it was fear, then lust which made you kiss that soldier? How, she asked me, can you not accept it? Do you think that fear or lust would preclude me from trying to save my family? Do you want to know which impulse predominated, which one finally pushed me toward the soldier and his mouth? Which impulse has made you challenge me just now, she asked me: was it fear, mistrust, lust, domination, desire? It's true, she said, we are grand creatures in some ways. Look at the way you have taken hold here, in an impossible quandary. But in other ways we are small and so often small-minded. We want to find one cause of a thing, to feel that we have knowledge or even control or at least understanding. I will tell you something else, because you deserve to hear it, because you are grand enough to hear it: I kissed that soldier because in that instant I fell in love with him. Yes. Love is something which we also can't understand. It was not a love I could think of pursuing. I fell out of love with him just as quickly as I fell in love with him. Why did I fall in love with him? Because of his good looks? Perhaps. Because I felt that above all he needed love at that moment and conveyed to me his need? Because of something I saw in his eyes? A sympathy? A fear? A sorrow? A strength of character? Because of a girlish fantasy for his uniform? Because in that moment when I felt everything was lost I needed to fall in love one last time? Because in that illuminated moment I could abandon myself to a foolish love, one I felt, but would not ordinarily pursue? Maybe. But Meleq is wrong. I did not abandon anyone or any belief. I abandoned my natural reserve. Do you remember the dance you and I did around each other when we first met, testing each other, questioning things, hesitating, waiting? With the soldier, all that went by the wayside. Meleq is wrong only because he doesn't understand life well enough. He thinks it can be contained but it can't. It's too much for that.

Of course I did not think I would write that. I did not think I would confide that secret to this paper. I wanted to confide it to someone, to anyone, to be relieved of its weight. But of course I couldn't. It meant that in some way the love that Alina had for me shared something with the kiss she had with that soldier, and until that moment I had despised that soldier. I have known too many of them, young men who think they are engaged in something noble when in fact they are hiding out from real life. Young men who use the cover of Governmental authority to vent their unacknowledged misunderstood furies. Young men frightened of or in need of or enamored of an authoritarian presence. Sentimental young men. Men like the President must have once been, so that now he is the Sentimental President, telling me about love, telling me that the work I'm engaged in is the work of a noble truth. Where is that young soldier now? What did he think of that kiss? Did he brag about it to his mates? Did it shatter him? Did he carry it into battle with him as a standard? I can see Alina's eyes, now, closely, the way they were when our faces were close. The way they were when we kissed. Was it love lust desire protection she felt for me? What quality distinguishes her momentary love for that young soldier from her love with me? Nothing? It's possible. In the presence of nothing in the absence of everything boundaries are dissolving. I don't like it, but there it is. Perhaps too I am embracing that young soldier, kissing him, pouring all my passion into an incongruous moment. Where I have to pour it now is here, into this writing which will not, likely, contain it.

Once I imagined the writing being found. Now I imagine it blowing away in a silence of the desert. After I die, after the last ounce of my ability has been exhausted. Will I have the presence of mind at that moment to go out, climb up to the bare hilltop where Alina once climbed, to let myself lean out, fall over? In a tribute not just to Alina but to that moment of what happened to her: that conjunction of despair and vitality so closely revealed, so that the tipping of the scale in one direction or another may depend on a literal grain of sand blown by an incongruous wind. Then my scale would tip just slightly in the opposite direction from which it tipped for Alina that day, and ooops, there I would go, to fall into eternity. This writing falling also out of my hands to be scattered by that same wind over the desert. Silence. In the desert canyons, on the desert floor. Each day the heat of the sun transmogrifying the pages into desert itself. What petrified letter would be the very last to become desert?

When once I said to Tassiossu, that night at Ynorob's after the poetry reading we had been to in the central plaza... oh, that poetry reading. Poet after poet getting up to that microphone, walking to the podium along that line they had set up of metal saucers flaming with wax and oil. Mostly bad poets, some good ones, some truly excellent poets requiring intense concentration to listen and even then feeling you would have to sit down with the thing yourself to get the juice of it out. So full we were of that poetry, talking about it, thinking about it, hearing it in our heads. That was the first night that Ynorob had run out of food. Had nothing to serve. Neither game nor root. Did everyone but me know that was the presage to disaster? Am I the last one to know am

I the fool's fool? Am I the only one who thought it was not such a problem, that we'd replenish supplies. I said to Abanno that we'd take care of it and he said to me, you know, boss, I don't know if I love you or envy you or pity you. No, no, I said, don't worry. We'll get food in here for Ynorob. He's a magician. Remember that night he made the most fantastic meal with nothing but mushrooms. Well, practically nothing. We stayed there, at Ynorob's, half the night. Drinking what beer we could scare up and water. Water! We didn't care. Well, we care, but we got past caring. That's how much we wanted to be there, talking, listening to the poets who'd come with us. Alina pointed to one of them she knew, Mr. Herd, saying that he knew all of Dante by heart. No! I protested. I don't believe it. Yes, Alina said, I know him. He knows all of the Divine Comedy. Mr. Herd himself was shy about it. Held up his hand as if to ward off our complimentary astonishment. But he gave in, delivering first a shy lecture on the section he would recite, then reciting for 20 minutes, in Italian which of course I didn't understand but, of course, didn't care. I think I got more out of it not understanding it. Not unlike one of Lucinda's concerts. The difference being that in Lucinda's concerts, strangely enough, I understood the language, which was the language of music. And, understanding the language, when I did hear music in my head at her concerts, or sounds from the environment as music, I was aware that I was straining to hear a certain sound I knew must be in there, but I had to stretch my senses to hear it. Even my sight, as I closed my eyes, if I could see that sound I could catch it with my sight then transmit it to my hearing. A sound beneath all the sounds you heard, or just beyond them. A music there, beneath the musics. But you'd never ever hear it. You'd know it was there sometimes, damnit, and you'd want to hear it. You'd want to go back over the whole concert again because you'd know you could find it. Not understanding the Italian of Dante gave me the feeling that whatever that unhearable music was, I was hearing it translated into words, recited by the poet, Mr. Herd. Not knowing Italian, I was satisfied with the belief that I had heard it. What extravagant creatures we are, and how abundant our desires. Then someone mentioned Meleq's text, the book whose one page he read over and over and over. *Meleq's Page* we called it. Meleq recited it slowly, as if it were a poem, as if it were the whole of the Divine Comedy.

Was it because of the hunger then that the fight broke out that night? Was there an edge because of the hunger that raised people's tempers? Later, talking about it with Abanno, we joked that Plato was right perhaps, there was something dangerous about poetry. Perhaps there is, although the poets were not much involved in the fight and in fact most of them were trying to stop it, one of them chanting some syllable of peace from his own region. Perhaps it helped finally to calm things down. Empouche was here by then? Yes. He was there. Oh, of course, that was the night he dazzled us all by his memory, by memorizing immediately Meleq's recitation from his page, then reciting it after Meleq. It was after the fight. Meleq himself cracked up laughing. He challenged Empouche to recite the Dante Mr. Herd had recited, and Empouche

actually began. We couldn't believe it. We held our breath.
He went on and on. We thought it must be some trick they
had cooked up together, but Empouche confessed that to give
himself something to think about as a soldier, to take his mind
off the battles, the drudgery of military life, he memorized some
of Dante to recite silently to himself while hiking, cleaning
equipment, during times of boredom. Then we all learned a
few lines of Dante in Italian. Can you imagine, a whole room
full of hungry, somewhat drunk citizens of the Emergency
Settlement, many of them sharply aware that the lack of food
at Ynorob's that night signaled impending catastrophe, reciting
Dante aloud together. In unison. What a sound. What a life I
am part of. Meleq stood up to proclaim that Mr. Herd was "the
Dante of the Emergency Settlement." Someone else proclaimed
Empouche "the Dante of the Emergency Settlement." I stood
up and proclaimed all the poets who had read that night as
"the Dantes of the Emergency Settlement." Even the bad ones,
I yelled, to everyone's huge laughter. But especially the good
ones. Applause. I bestowed on them all the Laurel Wreath of
the Emergency Settlement, an award which was still being
manufactured, but which would be delivered to each of them
at a public ceremony. And we did and I did, by God. Hwang
fashioned laurel pins from metal pilfered from collapsing
buildings, then I organized a ceremony in the Central Square
and in my presentation said that those poets were proof of the
fact that our survival did not depend on bread alone, for the
night of the poetry festival we had had no food at Ynorob's
restaurant, yet we had poetry. Someone from the audience

yelled out to know whether the bad poets were proof along with the good poets, and I said officially that yes, it must be so, to everyone's jocular approval. To close that ceremony Meleq recited his *Page*, holding the book as if he read from it.

It was in that discussion with Meleq about the *Page* that I came to some understandings, wasn't it? We sat in the café by my office. The whole Settlement had practically run out of coffee and tea. A few of the cafés had closed already. I told Meleq his *Page* was an excuse for not writing. If I want to quit writing, Meleq said, then I'll quit. I don't need excuses. What is it you're waiting to get from the *Page*? I asked him. I'm not waiting, he said. I'm getting it each time I read it, once or twice a day. I can't begin writing again until my understanding is saturated with the entirety of that one *Page*. Why not? I asked him. I've told you, he said. Tell me again, I said.

Until then, he said, something about writing was missing, something I don't know about writing. I protested: Look, I said, ignorance is part of the human condition. What you're trying to do is to cure ignorance with understanding. You've come to the point where you think you can do that and you've arbitrarily honed in on that *Page*. Leave the poor *Page* alone. Every day you will wake up with your ignorance again. You will read your *Page*, your ignorance will become apparent to you, you see some hole in your understanding, you think that you fill it, but it will become another hole somewhere else in your understanding. The next time you go to your reading you will think that you might just finally fill the last hole. But we are the holes, Meleq.

Yes, Meleq agreed with me. But (of course a but), he went on, I came to find out in pursuing this singular reading, that I can replace understanding with holes. When I am all holes then I will go back to writing.

I smile now to think of it. I looked at him then while a great smile grew on my face. What could one do with Meleq? I took his head in my hands, I kissed him on the cheek. He talked to me again about Rivka. Do you remember, he said, when I once told you how Rivka made me laugh? How that laughter invaded my resistance towards her? Let me explain it more. When I first met Rivka, I thought that love was something that would fill an emptiness. Oh, he said, a terrible emptiness from which I actually and truly suffered. By suffer I mean that each day it caused me not only pain, but disorder, disorientation, confusion. I had a huge hunger for love in my body, in my heart, in my head. When I met Rivka I saw immediately that the challenge was not to fill the emptiness with love, because to do that I would have to destroy Rivka. Do you see? Yes, I said. Were I to lose Rivka, he said, it's possible that I would go right back to my previous condition, so it is not a fact, that you cannot fill emptiness with love, it is a conundrum, because only in love can you not fill the emptiness with love. Outside of love, you will always imagine that you can.

It's similar with the *Page*, he said. I've chosen this *Page* precisely because it seems that from this *Page* there is something to be gotten. Something to be understood. To be known. When I'm all holes, then I'll start writing again. You'll see.

Now that I'm writing, while Meleq never began to write again, I see that he was wrong. He would never have become all holes. I have so much of Rivka's work here. Her sculptures, her paintings. That one painting, all shades of arcing black brush strokes along the long canvas, and in the middle one nearly dim, small whitish figure over which people disagreed so much, some saying it was a lonely and depressing figure, others that it was a strong and inspiring figure, and only Taïya saying once that it was both, putting an end to the discussion, for me at least. Many of Rivka's pieces were lost or destroyed in the crush, but some have remained. Most of them I've moved into my apartment or my office both for safekeeping and to have around me. Safekeeping for what? For when? Now am I as Meleq predicted I would be, hungry for something to fill a certain emptiness? With love here, my wife, or Alina, would even this be more tolerable?

That Alina foresaw the end. Could I find her? Has she survived? Well, she foresaw the end at the beginning. So that when she came to say goodbye, it was playing out a reality she had known would come. It is true that after she left I felt a greater emptiness than I'd ever felt. As though each object in the world around me, becoming emptied of her, became radically empty. Everything, large and small. The building, my apartment where we spent so much time together. The streets of the Settlement. Ynorob's. The Central Square. My pen. My body. Little things. A cup. A table. The Madonna in my office. My ideas. My idea of the Madonna. I had wanted to bring together Tassiossu's researches in the Madonna and Meleq's search in his *Page*. I tried to get them to talk it through one night in my office. A little mini-conference. But they were not the same, and I came to see it, though I couldn't, certainly, put my finger on it. I held out for a long time that night, convinced I could bring these two pursuits together. I wanted to do that, then hold a community symposium on it. When she came to say goodbye I asked why she was leaving just then. Because, she said, she didn't want to witness what was sure to happen to the Settlement: the bickering, the thievery, the desperation that would come. But there's nowhere else to go, I said. I know, she said, but at least we'll be off by ourselves, those of us from my village, who know each other so well, who all feel part of each other.

Why is it that time is bifurcated, doubled, by something like memory? Why is that memory, in order to escape something, in order to escape escaping, couples with continuum? What if memory occurred in a forgetful undenied present, that is, if memory occurred simultaneously with defense and with action as an aspect of the moment, of the present. What if that night I lay with Alina in my bedroom, the breeze coming in from the eastern window billowing the light curtains, letting them fall, then lifting them slightly again, then blowing into the room across our bodies, what if that night occurred in both the present in which it did occur, and at the selfsame instant, it occurred in memory. Violating the laws of physics. Now that night occurs only in memory, so that it's distant in time, and distant in my own mental geography. I mean the geography of a mind, physically. What if, writing now, as I sit here on a clear day, seeing the clear sky. Obliterations. Assassinations. The memory wants to insert itself in dominance now over reality. Poor, terrible, simple, absolute, perhaps even non-existent but purportedly evanescent reality, so maligned, bereaved, loved, sought after, deserted.

No, the present doesn't exist, we create it, invent it, name it. We memorize its details in order to recreate it, or in order to inscribe its existence on our bones with some very fine instrument. Memory, with all that it does to life. Washes it of pain to infuse it with the fragrance of its mistress, fulfillment. Or fills it with a pain larger than we might imagine—no, imagines pains larger than the significance of all time. If only I could have experienced certain things—that night with Alina, for example, that I keep coming back to—if I could have experienced it as reality and as memory at the same time, if reality were impregnated with memory so that the product of that union would be the actual birth of the creature, Life, which would swallow time so that it would appear conflated beginning inside ending as it did that night in Alina's dream as she recounted it to me the next morning: in her dream she witnessed the skyair in swirls of swift circular formations. Everything moving: moving in motion, moving in emotion. Beside her, on a rock, sat a creature (a kind of a man, she had said) who kept repeating some phrase she couldn't recall. Her dream of ending/beside (or inside)/beginning. I cannot remember now: did we make love that night before Alina told me about the invasion of her village, had we made love and I was languidly stroking the side of her body as she, turned

away from me, spoke? or had she told me of the invasion of
her village while I, in tension and sexual anticipation, stroked
the side of her body as she, turned away from me...? Had we
made love that night? I think yes. Wasn't that the night......?
no, that was another night. I remember the wind, though, she
had said to me that night: your hand on my body is rather like
the wind, they're both caressing me, and I said, yes, we're both
trying to sooth you, to calm you, as you tell your story. So there.
It must have been that we had already made love. Or that we
didn't make love at all that night. Because I was, I was trying
to sooth her, I was trying to calm her. I was trying to touch her
as I heard her story to calm myself. Having heard a hundred
such stories, having witnessed what I had seen, having already
known that my wife and my daughter were dead, when Alina
told me that story it was the most unbearable of all to hear. A
couple of times I wanted to take her whole body in my hand.
If I could stop Alina's story I could stop the whole history of it.
I caressed her body up / down, from her neck, just under her
ear, up and over the rise of her shoulder, then along the side
of her torso, down past her thigh. Then back again. A ritual
invented. A victory and a loss in the same motion. Having no
idea that later much later days later weeks later she would tell
me about having kissed the soldier on the porch. The Ninth
Soldier. Just now, in my imagination, I, too, grab the soldier,
garbed as he is in uniform, helmet, weapons, I kiss him full
on his mouth, I pull him to me. I take his crotch in my hand.
There. Why? I don't know why. There. Now we have both
done it, Alina. Come back, because now I understand you.

Now I want us to kiss, we two, you and I, Alina, who have both kissed the soldier on the porch of your family's house, have pursued him into the trance of a kiss.

You know, Tassiossu, that every evening here I have a ritual now. (Now I'm talking to you, Tassiossu. What if you actually, literally heard me wherever you are my dear good Tassiossu. What if you dreamt my words, dream their correspondent images. What is my desperation to be known, to be heard? To name you: Tassiossu. Then to be satisfied, or nearly satisfied.) Every evening, about half an hour before sundown, I have a drink. I'll tell you what I have left here: I have scotch, I have gin, I have whiskey, I have salvages of liqueurs in half a dozen bottles, I have two bottles of champagne. And the wine. I sit usually in the same spot, on the first rise to the north of town. You know the place. It takes me fifteen minutes to walk out there. I arrive usually about half an hour before sunset. I watch the sun go, I see the heat leave the earth's surface. Oftentimes, here, as you know, there will be few clouds, so the sunset will be pure, clarified, simple, direct. I sip the drink at this, my café, my country club. You and I, talking. No urgency pushing at us from behind. Sometimes I will sit on the edge of the rise, my feet dangling. I have never yet had an urge to let myself go over, the urge Alina once fought with, because here I am at ease, no matter what else. It is necessary, this pattern. From there I go back to prepare myself a meal. I am no Ynorob, you know that. But I act civilized. I take pleasure in the preparation. I focus only on the cooking. I work still from the stores we have of beans, rice, onions, flour, potatoes, canned fish, oils, dried tomato, dried herbs. It usually takes me at least an hour, although before I leave with my drink for the rise north of the town, I start the fire, so that by the time I'm ready to cook I have a fire going. I live, Tassiossu, with an absolutely limited supply of food and water. It is large yet, but it will never be replenished. Whatever I eat, whatever I drink, I eat and drink for the last time. Nothing will replace it. When it's all gone...well, it will take quite a while. I am only one. Only one, although, I'll tell you, I have had conversations with you while I've eaten. With Alina. With Abanno. With my daughter. My wife. Often, though, I eat quietly. I concentrate on eating. I have become an ascetic epicurean. Does that make sense to you? I can tell you accurately what I have eaten each night for at least the last ten or fifteen nights, if not further back. The ways I have combined simple things so that every night I'm curious to see how it works out. I have a running conversation in my head with my wife, who loved food, who loved to cook, about the dinners. I even think that I'm storing up all this information I've gathered because someday I'll report it to her, to her amusement and astonishment.

Sometimes I'll write in the late afternoon so that, while writing, I'll have the prospect of a drink and dinner in mind. I'll do that especially if I'm unsettled about the writing, anxious in doing it. That gives me something to keep me at work, thinking about dinner. How long do you think this writing will go on? Does it have some symbiosis with the food supply? Well, if there is no food certainly there will be no writing, but that's a problem writers have faced since the beginning of time

I imagine. Do you think, Tassiossu (yes, I am still talking to you), that the writers of, say, the Jewish or Christian Bibles had a hard time earning a living? In a way, if this manuscript is ever discovered, I would hope for it to be read like we read the Bible, as a text which came from no one knows where.

Now that I'm at it, shall I describe my daily life to you? To whom? To my wife? To Alina, who knew the physical properties of this, here, where I am now? To Tassiossu? To his Madonna? To begin then, at the beginning. A Day in the Life of the Emergency Settlement of the Western Quadrant, as told by its sole remaining inhabitant, the Governor. I get up each day early, just at dawn because I have always loved the dawn and I go on loving what I always loved bizarre how things do not change. I'm living in the same place, although I have the whole town I could go anywhere. Each day after I wash—using water storages—I go out to walk around because as always I'm never clear at first, as though something of the sleep world, the dream world still has a hold on me. Only the world outside my apartment can modify that. Each day it's a shock still to me that no one is there, on the streets, in the houses that are left standing. I walk to populate the Settlement. At first, sometimes I will feel that this is the severe isolation one part of me always feared that I lived in, always tried to escape. It is unreal. Then I will have to contemplate what is real, what is unreal, to conclude over and again that the real is the expected, the habitual. Nothing more than that, so that the real as we always called it is always subject to cancellation. Even in a world where it is bizarre how things do not change.

I like to walk most—as I always did here—among the ruins of the great buildings. Because I imagine prolific life there? Because the cessation of a tumultuous sound makes what we call the silence more audible, although of course it's not truly silence, it's the presence of the most minute sounds. Sometimes I will stop to imagine I hear the Pythagorean concertos. Remember, Abanno, the night we sat with Lucinda as she told us about Pythagoras? What I hear when I stop, on those morning walks, to listen like that, is the sound of my breath my heart and those Pythagorean songs sometimes assonant sometimes dissonant sometimes they are the sound of my blood. But I should describe the streets, writing for my wife, who was never here. Some of the collapsed buildings were great old stone structures. Some of them survived from antiquity, until now. Some were quite new, full of steel which doesn't hold up as well in ruin as stone does. I will find stone walls to sit on, or intersecting sections of walls defining what were once rooms. Now there is the irregularity of shape, the animation of interplay in the chance configuration of the way things fell. Among these ruins people made lives. I will pass by where, on my first day here, I saw the boy and girl with their coffee. Now there's an event—I am about to run out of coffee. When that happens, in about ten days I think, I will have to mark it with some sign. I will have hot water still, I will look for ways to make teas.

Sometimes, walking in the old neighborhoods, I'll pass by certain houses where people whom I knew lived, where particular things occurred. Where we met Empouche, for example. Yesterday I was there. It's a narrow street with small, single houses on it, and one brick apartment building. The temperature was cool, there was still a dull dew on the lawns, on the trees. We were up against the apartment house, our hands against the cool brick, our feet pulled out by kicks Empouche delivered to our calves. He paced around behind us, came up beside us, kicked out our feet an inch more, paced again behind us, short, quick steps. I could tell he was watching the street, up and down. I thought he would kill us. That's what I felt from him, that he would burst out with his gun, that he had to, that we were dead already. What would I feel, physically? My breath came short yet heavily, an odd combination, a biological paradox. Deep, quick breathing. If you were to keep that up it feels like you'd faint. I didn't. Neither did I when I breathed that same way, for an even longer time, when I heard about Empouche and Alina. Sitting in that old wooden chair with the black fake leather seat at the Café Noumenchlature, the way my arms rested on the wooden chair-arms, my fingers interlaced in my lap. That breath then coming from a different body, not my own, my own body then absent of breath, relieved of it. The waterworks had been in progress then. It had begun. We'd been discussing cartage. Had Empouche thought the squads we'd had him organize later during the raids against us had ever any chance of succeeding?

But I'm drifting, where today I have a specific writing task I've given myself. Maybe it'll take a few days. After coming back from my morning walk I'll make coffee and breakfast. For breakfast I'll have remains of last night's dinner. I'll always make enough the night before, at least of the grains, be it rice, or potato, or the flatbread, although I haven't made that for a while. Maybe I will again. For a change. No, let's back up. When I get back from my morning walk I'll get a fire going for the coffee and food. That takes a bit of time, during which usually I'll read. All the books we had here, some I've gathered from others' houses. Tassiossu's papers, I've read through all of those. While reading in the morning I'll come across the same question drifting: how can it be? How can this be? How can it be, for example, that I knew Tassiossu, that he lived here with me, that he fled in one of the later attacks, leaving behind everything so that he left with less than he came with, and that I now sit here reading his papers, his researches on the Madonna? This is not a philosophical issue, a metaphysical question, a linguistic analysis: it's a kind of child's question, a petition asked more in the eyes that in the mind. Usually now I cook outside. By the time I get back from my walk the sun will be breaking up the moisture, the coolness abating, although sometimes I'll sit close to the fire. This morning for example, I did that, reading from Tassiossu's papers for a while. Then I went in to get one of Meleq's books, came back out and imagined which page of it might be the one Meleq fixated on. I read three pages at random. It could have been any one of them. I went back into the apartment. From the box of Tassiossu's papers I took a folder marked "M. Differentiation." From what I could tell, they are notes regarding the small differences in Madonnic representations, discussing what they signify. He was writing about Da Vinci's unfinished *Adoration of the Magi,* the abjection of the Magi compared with the curious gaze of other figures. There is a reproduction of it in the folder. He compares the whole painting to another, a Buoninsegna altarpiece in which all those surrounding the Madonna and Christ gaze on in rapture. The difference in the Madonna herself, Tassiossu writes, is that in the Da Vinci she is adoring, beautiful, whereas in the earlier Buoninsegna she is more severely drawn, more absent in expression, less attractive as a woman. Indeed, Tassiossu writes, her cloak is more voluptuous than she is. But, he goes on, because Da Vinci never finished his drawing, the Christ Child—more an adult-infant than a baby—has been given shaded in darkness, whereas the Madonna is as yet all light, in orangish hues and glows. Tassiossu calls her the Madonna as Yet Unmanifest on Earth, and later the Madonna Ever Coming Into Being, and later the Madonna About To Be Known. Then he goes off onto a discussion about works of art and time. Time, Tassiossu writes, is one of the authors of a work of art. It is time that fragmented the poems of Sappho, written in the 7th Century, lost by the Middle Ages, retrieved from papyri. So that in the 7th Century the Greek world had the poems of Sappho, whereas now time has changed those poems so that what we have is a form of fragmentation with time as the author. Tassiossu goes into all of this because of what time, or circumstance, did to Da Vinci's drawing. What we have now, Tassiossu says, is not an unfinished drawing so much as a different drawing, a drawing of the Madonna Perpetually in Formation. You see, I could have been an artist, a scholar, a professor spending his morning reading about the Madonna of Da Vinci and the poetry of Sappho and the nature of art and theories of fragmentation and time as I sip coffee in a café. I'm not. I wait for the fire to be ready for cooking. Then I begin with the coffee, making it in the small metal espresso pot I had brought with me, then heating up the rice with onions and dried hot peppers in a pan which hangs from a hook I've constructed over the fire, a little oil in the bottom of the pan.

I eat outside. The claustrophobia of eating alone indoors. Impossible. In the rain, I eat on the porch. In the cold, I'll eat inside, but usually just standing at the counter in the kitchen. I have no Sappho. I would read her if I did. I remember the clarity of her lyric, the fluid simple suppleness of it, even in translation. I would read her aloud. To myself. Sometimes I think to myself: look, you have constructed here a life of basics, an uncomplicated existence. This morning I was thinking that. Before I fell asleep after breakfast. I usually nap after breakfast.

Is it interesting to you, the description of my day? Can you picture it? Alina. You have survived. You were the most durable person I have ever known. When I came back from the first visit with the President you were the one who urged me to make plans for a separation, who supported me most in my belief that soon we would be cut off altogether by the Capital. Who most saw with me that we could find ways to go on. Even when Abanno began to fear it.

Walking back from the meeting, the eight of us: Lucinda, Alina, Meleq, Guillemette, Abanno, Grammatico, Tassiossu,

Rivka. About 11 o'clock. Dark dark. Walking along Avenue Gruppo delle Macchine. Because Lucinda had her violin with her I suggested the idea: why not stop here for a time, I said. Would you give us a concert here, Lucinda, out here? Where? she asked, just here, in the street? No, I told her, over there, in the ruin. We'll sit on the half-pedestals of fallen columns, on the chewed up remains of walls, on the ground itself. I urged her, until she complied. All right, she said, a concert in the ruins. No, I said, don't think of them as ruins. Think of them as structures: we humans, we built them one way; time has edited them: this is what they are now: structures extant.

I sat on a collapsed pillar. Grammatico sat on the ground next to me, on my right. Abanno sat on the remains of a wall. Tassiossu stood, leaning against what had been a portal. Alina sat at the foot of the pillar-end I sat on, leaning half against the pillar, half against my legs. Tassiossu sat down on a huge rock. What it was doing there, no one could fathom. Rivka stood at first, in front of us, to introduce Lucinda, as Lucinda unpacked her violin.

> Lucinda, Rivka said, is an extraordinary musician who has influenced my own painting. At first when I heard her concerts, I thought she was literally playing the unknown. That's what I was after in my own painting, I thought, some sense of what cannot be known. Soon,

however, I realized that Lucinda was playing absolutely and perfectly the known, the completely known, and nothing more. Nothing more could be played. The completely known: vast as it is. Disillusioning as it is. Limiting as it is. Limitless as it is. Enlightening as it is. With its propensity to elude us. That's how I wanted to paint, I thought. The literal playing of music seems always to suggest the unknown. I don't know why. The way Lucinda plays, suggests the known. I wanted to suggest the known in my painting in a similar way. No...no. That's all wrong. I'm mistaken. Let me start again. From somewhere else. Lucinda's playing includes the unknown, it straddles the known and the unknown. Her work reduces the sum of all our realities to the moment of playing. Because the moment I began to paint, influenced by Lucinda's music, the world of the known, I found myself alluding to the unknown. Or this: as we listen to Lucinda's music we hear the known world go by: the sounds around us, our own thoughts, the sounds of our bodies, our feelings. But we watch Lucinda. The stillness of her instrument. And we imagine there something else: something beyond all these things floating by us. If only Lucinda would pick up her violin, draw the bow across one string one time, we would know everything we need to know. But she keeps us harbored, anchored. Even as we float off on our thoughts. Well, I meant only to make a sort of joke of an introduction, but look what I've done. I don't know what I've said. I tried to say something very specific about Lucinda's work, about what it's done to my work, but I don't know what I've said. I meant to say only how funny Lucinda's concerts are, how they amuse me, make me laugh. I'm going to listen very carefully now, because I thought I had understood this work, but I realize I'm still confused about it. How can a violin sitting still on someone's lap confuse me?

Lucinda sat on the edge of a wall, smiling. Lucinda came forward, put her arm around Rivka, kissed her cheek. Rivka withdrew to the wall where Lucinda had left her violin case. Lucinda sat down on a chair Abanno had gotten for her from a café around the corner while Rivka had spoken. She set the violin, strings down, on her lap; she set the rosined bow on her lap between the violin and her torso. She took a deep breath, as you might see a pianist do, before beginning. Again, like a pianist, she shook out her hands, cracked her fingers lightly intertwining them in the fingers of the opposite hand, shook them out again, put them down in the space left between the bow and her torso, and you could see that the piece had begun. I continued to watch Lucinda, stare at her actually. This time I was trying to fathom what was transpiring in Lucinda's mind, in her body, in her hands. What music was she hearing? All the possible musics: Mendelssohn's violin concerto, or some Hungarian melody of Franz Liszt, transcribed for violin, or one of the African Songs of Kaje Nbono, or John Cage's $4¢33^2$ [the original inspiration for her concerts, she had told us once, lecturing to us on music]. Then I watched her body, her straight, performer's posture, her breathing relaxed and complete. I saw in her an impulse to pick up the violin, to begin playing. Then I saw her body, without moving, go through a whole scenario: her mind and her body were throwing a tantrum, like a child. She wanted to pick up the violin to play, but wouldn't allow herself to do it. Those two impulses warred. She was smiling. The brash child became difficult, screaming at Lucinda, then withdrew into a pouting, hurt, defensive crouch. Meanwhile the silent vigilance of the adult Lucinda sat patiently. This passed through her. Her eyes looked at no one of us in particular, although sometimes she would look around, seeing each of us in turn. When she saw me so intently watch her, she didn't acknowledge my stare: she neither accepted it nor complained of it. Her breathing moved in a mostly regular, soft rhythm, although occasionally a deeper breath punctuated it. We had no spotlights here, of course; we saw her was only in the natural light. We all sat close to her, but when she bent her head down to look at the violin, her thick short dark hair blackened that part of her altogether so it no longer existed. I still saw the violin, at which she would look sometimes for a long time. I saw her chest still, the red shirt that she wore that night, her inhale and exhale moving her chest and her stomach, raising her slightly with each inhale, letting her down with each exhale. Once, I glanced down at Grammatico, who sat with his legs pulled up to his chest, his arms around them. I saw only the top of his head. What was he thinking about, doing, what thoughts plagued him or pleased him? What music? Likewise, from time to time, Alina would rub along my leg with her hand. I would put my hand on top of her head. I would hear her voice speak something. I hear it now, in her absence. Her voice is an object she has left behind. Mostly that night I focused my attention on Lucinda, on her body, her eyes, on her mouth, her chest, on her lap, on her violin as it sat in her lap. She turned the violin so the strings faced up, then, after a few minutes, turned it back down again. About five minutes later, I would say, although who can say how much time passes in such a circumstance, she turned the violin up again. This time I had actually felt the strings squashed against her lap, claustrophobic. When she returned the strings to the air they relaxed, expanded. Just at that point, when the violin became most at ease, I had a paradoxical vision: I saw an army of thousands in chariots come tearing into this Settlement, set fire to everything. I looked around at each one: Lucinda, Alina, Abanno, Grammatico, Tassiossu, Rivka. Each one yet safe. No one on fire. No one terrified.

I have never-ending time now to think, yet I wish only to hear Lucinda play her violin. To see her do it. The tones I imagine she could get from that wood. It just occurs to me now, with a pang of anxiety, that this writing is somewhat like Lucinda's playing. No. Wrong. Lucinda had an audience. The whole Settlement. My audience is gone. This is not a silent text. Thank God I'm not an artist, like Lucinda, like Rivka, who went back to her work in a confusion I don't think she ever clarified. I'm just a diarist without need for a guiding philosophy. I'm writing for reasons I can't explain, so have no need to acquit my work, to construct an apologia, to affect anything with the writing. I write for nothing except perhaps for the sake of each word coming into being. Yesterday I went back to the caves, stood there, spoke aloud. Why, I asked the ancient hand-artist of the cave, did you make this image? Clear figure that it is, in enduring pigment, its color depending on the light, done in blue. I spent a lot of time rummaging around there, actually, yesterday. Spent the night in the cave, to see what it might feel like to live that way. I still have an apartment, I still have a bed, I still have pen and paper, and ink.

After breakfast (are you listening?), usually I'll fall into a short nap. My dual relationship to dreams: I look forward to the release they might offer me, and I fear them. It was Alina who pulled me out of the dream about the President. That was one of those dreams—there's a word for them, what is it?—dreams so vivid that you wake up still dreaming. It was after my trip to the Capital. In that dream, I left the President's Office, then I passed through an outer office where an official reclined on a couch reading something, some papers. They thought I had gone out the second door, the outer door, and left the offices, but I hadn't closed that second door yet. The President screamed his head off at that poor bastard: Take your fucking feet off that fucking couch or I'll have your head! I'm confusing things. That did happen, didn't it? What an awful dream. Can I be confusing dream and event? Alina tried to calm me. It's a way of defusing the shock you had from the President, she said, it's a natural process. I told her that the President hadn't yelled at anyone like that. Yes, she said, he had yelled like that. It happened. Had it? I think it had.

After breakfast I'll usually fall asleep. It's a great luxury. How odd that I came to enjoy something like this only at the expense of losing everything, everyone. After I wake up from my morning nap I'll clean up from breakfast, look at my manuscripts, read, go for a hike. Yesterday, for example, I hiked out to the waterworks. Abanno's masterpiece. It's all there still, believe it or not. The entire mechanism of collection pits, fire pits, pots, incipient pipelines. We had a great time, Abanno, you and I, talking over the plans for that thing. We were like some great old industrialists full of dreams. What we created of each other while creating the water-works—that was the masterpiece, no? That's what can't exist now, yes? What time does to *that* masterpiece. I was looking at the plans last week, after I came back. I spent a night up there, Abanno, as we used to do. Now it's become an earthworks in sculptural shapes, an art piece. Even in my isolation now, there is a stillness up there emphasized by all that equipment sitting quiescent, inactive. One human being among it all, seeing it, coming back to write it. Now as I remember it there is something about it that language refuses. I can say: there was a large pot, four feet high, three feet in diameter, suspended over a fire pit by a system of pulleys which ran wires horizontally and vertically and at various angles over and across that pot, over and through the whole waterworks, cutting the space of the waterworks into squares, triangles, cubes. Yet what if I also say: the objects are in relation to each other, the pots, for example, the hoses. They rearrange themselves from time to time. All those objects in their tension make a statement of some kind. It's that statement that I tell you about, Abanno, so that you can sense it because you made it. At night all those objects take on a different quality. Then I wanted to tell you that it's not even about the objects themselves there, Abanno, it's more primary: it's about light. And the absence of light. It was late, dark by the time I got back, so I was looking at the plans by candlelight. Pages of drawings with all their visions and revisions. You were assiduous, Abanno. You would get potable water to a village of fifteen thousand from the mountains, across the desert floor, into the village. The drawings themselves smelled of our meetings. I almost looked up from perusing them because I heard your voice say something. Do I exist now, without you, without Alina, without Rivka and Meleq, the way those pots and those pulleys and those pits exist on the hillside. Am I an object whose peripatesis is just quicker and larger than those pots, pulleys, pits. I suppose that from some perspective, indeed I am, and that from some greater perspective I too am utterly quiescent.

So after a morning nap (I'm trying to tell you about my day, about what I do now, about what's here. I apologize for the distractions) I'll read, walk around, think, fix what can still be fixed. I won't start writing until later. Why? I don't know, but it's important not to start writing yet in the day. It's even a pleasure to restrain myself from doing so. (A pleasure Lucinda knew?) It's important now, too, to get this part down, this description of my ordinary activity. Why? So that I can incorporate you (a changing you: at one time my wife, at one time Abanno, at one time Grammatico, at one time Tassiossu, at one time my daughter—probably my favorite choice, actually —) into this life, incorporate myself out of it? Establish it? I don't eat much for lunch, often nothing again until dinner.

This is the time of day I exercise. Then I do my biological research. Remarkable, yes? With no training in hard sciences I have become expert on the living organisms here. I catalogue all those I find, naming each one. Plants, insects, small animals, weeds. I am building a system of knowledge. It is a dialogue I maintain with my surroundings, with what once was the Emergency Settlement of the Western Quadrant, and which is now a collection of spiders, ants, cacti, water-bearing plants, flies, flowering plants. What little I know of science! I remembered: first you have genus, then family, then species, then individual. I think. Is that it? I'm trying to find the relations by establishing a basis for doing so. That's the most difficult part, without training. What a real scientist would think of my names!: Coy, for a flowering cactus which blooms for a few hours, late in the day, and then loses its blossom by dawn; Nervioso for an ant species I've found, brownish, which zigzags a lot on the return trip to its ant hill. Tiny White Pendiculus for a tiny flower whose head leans downward. (Should it be Pendiculum?) Names like that. As I've named certain stars, invented constellations. Written it all down, with diagrams. It occurs to me just now that I'm not only building a system of knowledge, but a whole encyclopedia, aren't I? Constellations named for my daughter, for my wife, for my father, for Alina, for Tassiossu, one named Lucinda which resembles a musical instrument of some kind or other. Writing it now makes me laugh. Have I really done all this? I never stopped to think about it. One person can culture a culture. But for whom? For only himself. No. Don't think about it. It will all go the way of this manuscript, eventually. I suppose the whole thing is a culture, yes? The naps each morning, all of it. I do keep imagining, can't help imagining that someday someone will arrive. I'll take them into my office. From the desk drawers beneath the Giotto Madonna I'll pull out sheets of biological descriptions, botanical topography, crude drawings, sample leaves, stones, charts of star movements with lists of astronomical data, astrological neological names. Along with the calendars I've devised which mean nothing because they correspond to nothing outside of here. They don't mark weeks or years, even, they only mark sightings of certain botanical phenomena on which I'm charting circularity. No doubt I would have a grand time explaining all this to Alina, who would look on amazed, proud of me, delighted to have all this exquisitely detailed graphic description of this place we lived in together, excited to think that she can peruse all this and compare it to the reality around us. No doubt I have thought of showing it all to my daughter as a way of giving her an introduction to so much that we have of life. Laying it out in front of her. Saying to her: Here it is. It is all yours. Showing it all to Tassiossu who would come scraggling in here from the wilderness, driven again on some course of exile he managed, again, to survive. I'd nurse him back from dehydration, from starvation, from dementia, delusion. I'd bring him back by letting him thumb through his old notes, his photographs, his researches. Then I'd spread out my work for him. Look at what we had here all the time, Tassiossu, that we talked mostly about survival, mostly about your Madonna, mostly about the culture that had brought us to be living in the Emergency Settlement of the Western Quadrant. All that time we discussed my work as a Bureaucrat holding together a social structure that was doomed by the very people who sent me here originally to hold it together. Better that all along I should have mapped the stars and the plants, yes?

Tassiossu had brought in plants from outside the Settlement to decorate my office. (Notice how your manuscript has changed: how now you are talking to that mythical substance again: the audience, the reader. Myth, though, grows out of reality, no? Enlarges on it. So what is this small entity, the reality of it, the reader?) He would go on walks frequently, always taking a spade with him to dig up things he'd found. We'd pot them, tend them. Guillemette, coming over frequently, would cart some off to her place. She was planning another show into which she would incorporate a lot of these plants. The raids had begun by that time, by the time she had started talking about another performance. We could never determine who they were, were they our own Government's forces, or were they someone else, some of the enemy's forces, or random roving gangs? They would run through the streets, fifteen or twenty of them, enough to cause enough panic to drive everyone almost insane with fear. They would always manage to kidnap a few people, whom we'd find dead the next day out in the desert somewhere.

In that I failed as a Bureaucrat. The failure to prevent those attacks. Empouche and I worked on it endlessly. Tactics upon tactics. Meetings. Armaments. Ideas. Organization. Preparedness. What do I think? I think they were from the Government and the Government wanted to destroy us, to disperse us, we were a nuisance to them. What do I think? I think they were a pestilence. What do I think? I think they were the ultimately refined distilled essence of the worst most depraved most corrupt most degenerate most venal most egregiously incarnate possibility of the human form. What do I think? I think they were truly from another world, because nothing on this earth could have been that vicious, malignant, malevolent. What I think hardly matters because it happened. What I thought was useless to stop them. What I thought could not stop the Settlement's inhabitants from leaving. I thought for a time that they were a special squad of the President sent especially to torture me for my continuous letters of request (which I'm sure he never saw), for my letters upbraiding him (which I'm sure he never saw), for the letter I finally sent laying the fate of my wife and my child on his conscience (which I'm sure he never saw), on the conscience of a man so out of touch that he likely had no conscience, a man who had constructed a mind of self-justifications so arcane, so self-serving, so enmazed that conscience was successfully circumvented by a system so circuitous as to make the complexities of our waterworks amateurish. What do I think? I think they came, over and over, I think they outsmarted us, deceived us, outfoxed us, over and over. I'm not one of those to think, if only we had done this, if only we had thought of that, if only we'd had such and such a weapon, such and such a tool. There is what happened, there continues to be what happened. There continues to be the day Alina came to say good-bye. There continues to be the death of Empouche. There continues to be the departure of Guillemette with the whole Gruppo. There continues to be my refusal to leave, my inability to leave, my fear of leaving, the fact that I have not left. That I was not killed. That they stopped coming. There was nothing more to come to. There continues to be the fact that I do not know what happened to the boy and the girl I saw on my first day. Were they killed? Did they escape? Who were they? Were they alone? I have actually thought, writing this manuscript—writing written by hand—that I should write a story about them, that I should satisfy myself by creating a fiction of their lives. I'm not a writer like that. I wouldn't do it justice. I would fall into sentimentalities, trip over too many narrative problems. You would have to abandon yourself to the characters themselves. I could not successfully imagine another person like that. I wouldn't want to just write their story. I prefer the story of the performance of the Gruppo delle Macchine Imaginare. Something which has a life of its own, apart from reality, at the heart of reality. No. There is no "heart of reality"? I prefer the journal. It's enough for me.

When I am gone, by whatever means I go now, it will be a sort of triumph. There will be no one to look for the heart of reality, no one to describe the ruins, to talk about it all. No one to preserve the stones, consider the success or failure of a water works. Above all, no one to remember what happened here, let alone what happened there, in the Capital, in the villages. No one to interfere with the existence of things. No one to define them, describe them. The things themselves. I can imagine that I am already gone. There. Now. It doesn't matter at all that the ruin of the stone statue of the young boy rescued from the terrace of somewhere and placed in the courtyard of the Café Noum has parts of its stone torso chipped away, that three of its toes are missing, that the curls of its stone coif are half mangled. My absence, already accomplished just now and maybe long overdue acquiesces in existence. It acquiesces even in my own existence.

Or, no, that won't do, will it? For a minute I stopped here, after what I just wrote, and thought, well, there, that's it. I looked around me, where I sit now on the patio of the small building of my apartment, the patio where I write now so frequently. I looked around at the building, at the window to my apartment bedroom (now seen from the opposite viewpoint, so that I might look at it now and, given the nature of things, Alina and I might even be at the same time up there, inside, lying in bed, talking), at the plants that surround me in their planters, at the wooden fence to the north, at the Settlement itself to the south. All right. That's it. No more. But it isn't "no more," and why? Because it can't be? Because it won't be? It? What? The words? What are they if not objects like the apartment window, the fence to the north, the plants in their planters as I've planted them. As Alina and I have planted them. I'm Adam with a name, a word for each thing: Planter. Plant. Window. Curtain. Alina. Crisis. Each word comes so easily, as if from muscle, sinew, tissue, bone. Speak to me. Please speak to me. Is that what I write for, now, readerless as I am, so that I be spoken to? But it is I who speak. No? I who write these words: Abanno, Tassiossu, my wife, Meleq, Rivka, violin. Crisis. No. Stop. No more. I can't take any more. I don't go on. I end. Finally I end. No more. Yes to no more. Thank you. The tired man thanks you.

No more? What a joke. Look at what you wrote yesterday:

No More. Yes. More more. In that ending was your beginning if ever. Most of the day yesterday you believed it, didn't you? No more. No more indeed. Whom are you fooling? Can't kid a kidder, eh? Come on, knock it around, words on a page. Tassiossu, give me more Tassiossu, living and breathing. Argue with him: say: Tass: what would you make of the stone statue with the missing toes and the curtailed coif? Speak to me, damn you, Tassiossu. The way you are wont to do. Say to me: Well, let's talk about a damaged Madonna. All right. Do you know the one, Tassiossu will say, have I described for you the ancient wooden Madonna who is missing both arms so that the baby sitting in her lap would fall, were it not carved wood. Have I told you about it? It comes from about the 11th Century. Very early. It is the same thing as I was talking to you about before, about Da Vinci, about how time is one of the creators of our works of art. In this case (yes, Tassiossu, that's it, go on, talk) of the Madonna, in the 11th Century the sculptor gave us a statue in which the Child sat embraced in all the security of the Mother's arms. Time has carved us a statue much more to the taste of our modern mood: the Child sits in contingency balanced on her leg for as long as he keeps his own balance, open to any wind, about to fall, already fallen. The original is in a museum in Jerusalem, having been carried there from Europe by a French Crusader who lost his life on that expedition. I call it the Modern Madonna. Or sometimes Free Falling Christ. She has let him go, he will adventure on to his own fate. Sometimes, looking at my photographs of it, I've seen her, the Madonna, move her phantom limbs around him, to protect him again. Sometimes I've seen that time, which took away her arms, also re-carved her face to add an astringent serenity. If she moves, she would surely throw him off her lap. Usually scholars (according to Tassiossu) write about the statue when it left France in 1086, bound for the Holy Land (land of Perpetual Emergency and Ever Abiding Settlement?), in its presumptive wholeness, with its arms intact.

I asked Tassiossu would he lecture on that in the Settlement lecture series, as he had done on other Madonna topics. He agreed, he was eager to do it, had begun preparing notes, but we never got around to that lecture. The raids had begun, although we were still sure then that we could repel them. In fact, Empouche borrowed that Madonna/Child image from Tassiossu as an emblem for his defense squads.

No. No. Go on talking about your daily life now. It's important, for some reason. To tell someone. All right. After my nap, in the early afternoon, I'll garden. Cactus have become my expertise. I have Barrel Cactus, Star Cactus, a few whose names I knew, most whose names—Latinate and common—I've invented: Butterfly Cactus, Manuscript Cactus, Nightingale Cactus, Blue Invitational Cactus, Laughing Cactus, many, many. I've grown two fanning palms in the courtyard, so on and so on. Each of these I've entered in my taxonomies with an entry indicating the three names I have given them (species, family, individual), where I got them from, when I first planted them, how fast they've grown (with no ruler to be found I measure by lengths comparable to the first joint of my left index finger, and I've called this measurement a "joint," so something will be 4 1/2 joints, 6 joints, etc. It makes me think, actually, of the way we had renamed the streets in the Settlement after local events or people: I name the size of my plants after my own most local of measurements), their colors, variations of color, changes of color. The amount of water and sunlight each one requires. I move them around, rearrange them.

And thus, the early afternoons. I have sat on the patio looking at my plants, just observing them. I've carried a few of them, one at a time, out into the surrounding desert, set them up on a small rise or at the edge of a curve or even in the midst of a flat plane to see how they might interact with the landscape. Fecund desert. Intriguing how they add a clearly man-made quality. To my mind. Not to the landscape's mind, surely. When I walk by the same place afterwards it is then marked for me, so that I'll stop to look at it, assess it, see how it redefines the shape of things around it. Bring it water if it needs. These placements remind me somewhat of the hand in the cave. Once, in the cave, Lucinda said: Imagine this cave, she said, just before this handmark was put here. Thousands of years ago, just before, the day before, the hour before. About a month later, she gave a concert inside the cave. At noon. About fifty people came. Her following by that time. She gave the concert in the first interior chamber, not near the hand, which was further in. Was it because we were enclosed in the cave? I looked around during the performance. I stood up, leaned against the cave wall for a while, then stood straight, without any support, just watching the people who had come, so many of whom I knew. That was the time I felt so afraid, that fear was the music I heard. It was all I heard that day. The music of my own fear, I suppose, if you would call it that. It wouldn't leave me, that fear, but came in waves with the intervals between each wave not long, not filled with anything else, so that although I call it waves of fear, it was a continuum also, a continuous fear. Is emotion wave or particle? I could tolerate that fear within Lucinda's performance, her violin on her lap anchored me to the moment. Despite the impulse to walk out into the clear air to shake off the fear, I didn't move— because of the violin. Staring at it. We are in ruins, things are getting worse, what is there to fear? Almost everything which could happen had happened. Could I detect any clue in Lucinda's face of the same fear. Was it coming from her. I couldn't tell. Did others feel it, Guillemette, for example, fearless Guillemette? Again, I couldn't tell. Could I find release through communion with others. That concert went on for a long time, my fear went on for a long time. Did you feel fear that day, during that concert? I asked Alina. Alina looked at me, watched my face, but didn't answer. I couldn't insist, ask her again. I took her silence as assent, as an inability to talk about it, but of course I could be completely wrong.

At the end of each day's writing I will choose one word from the day's work as a marker: today it will be this word: "assent."

A couple of days ago I spent the afternoon staring at the poster of the Giotto Ognissanti Madonna, the one Tassiossu left hanging in the office. The office was dusty, I had been cleaning, got tired, sat down, stared at the poster. It's painted on wood. The Madonna here sits on a sort of throne, a wooden structure painted in reds and yellows, an arched wooden triangular structure over her head. Two wings, each with a window cut into it, swing out at either side of her, encasing her. Two steps lead up to the daïs, where she sits. On either side of her a green-robed, haloed figure holds one wooden wing by a sort of pedestal at the bottom of each wing, so these angels might swing the wings closed, or pull them further open. These angels hold them gently still. They have just opened them so we might see her better, they are showing her to us. Madonna and the Child on her lap. His small hand raised in a gesture of—what? of discourse, though he would give us a word, the word. Would it be creation would it be destruction? His hand raised against the backdrop of her breast, lightly sheathed in a white gown with gold trimming, through which, her breasts— now that, tired, I sit here gazing—can be seen. This is the voluptuous, most feminine part of her. She wears a dark cloth, a full-length deeply black cloth with a single gold stripe in it, the whole of it edged in gold; it covers her head. Does this dark suggest the coming crucifixion of the Child, to foretell death, or the unknown, is it emblematic of the dark side of the Great Mother in which the Child colludes? Is the dark cloth enveloping her a luscious complement, physical, sexual? The visibility of her breasts, now that I see it, draws you perhaps beyond that dark cloth, as the shape of her breasts is revealed where the cape falls away, exposing the white diaphanousity of her gold-hemmed gown. The Child's raised hand draws my attention, set between the breasts, about a foot away from her body. The hand of the Madonna on the Child's leg. A secret which the wings would close to hide were we to look too closely? Yet the window cut into each wing, so that, were they closed, much would still be revealed. Roughly reddish colors throughout. Two angels kneeled at the bottom step. Her eyes, narrow. Was that a convention, Tassiossu? Small black eyes, long thin nose, reddish lips neither quite set nor yet relaxed. Ten figures (Madonna, Child, two angels, two door/wing bearers, four witnesses) haloed, six citizen-witnesses unhaloed. And who are they? I looked at them. Bearded men, Roman-faced women. Do not close the doors, I address those attendants, do not shut the secret on me, the inevitable closing of these doors/side-wings, the scene retreating from my eyes before I can see too much, before I can see either what I need to see or what it is clear I need not see. The whole painting set in a rectangular-sided frame, except that at the top (as in the painting itself an arched triangle sits above the Madonna's head), the frame comes to a triangular roof.

Yesterday I sat. Looking at it for God knows how long. I couldn't stop looking. If I stopped looking those side-wings would close. The gold background. Those quietly, deeply colored tones from the early 14th Century, far from here. Those reds which aren't bright, but have a strong presentation. The black of that cloth in which I see purple. How can I read this Madonna, Tassiossu? Except to say: do not close those wings. Although as I watched it, the wings were already long ago closed. Had been. I was seeing a moment in time which didn't truly exist, a moment seized out of time, reserved. If I had articulated those words: if I had made them concrete: "do not close those wings," I would have dismembered that moment ex-time, only time would be left. So I did not speak them. They exist inside that painting. If it has survived. What has survived all this? Everything? For a time, as I sat there, my eyelids became the wings on either side of the Madonna. There is no one to betray. Tassiossu, I would like to sit with you in the office as I sat a few days ago, the two of us, for hours, for the whole day (it got dark while I sat there, cool and dark), not talking about the painting at all. The frame is all gold, except for one thick red line of what looks like a separate piece of wood inlaid into it. She does not get up, Tassiossu, she does not move, they do not close the wings. I can't make head or tails of this painting, Tassiossu, I can only sit there as I did a couple of days ago looking at it. Now I don't know what it's doing to me, with me, for or against me. I don't know what it means. I don't know what you were looking for, ultimately. Your search. Here she is, Tassiossu. Have a look. All your passion for her: infantile, transcendental, sexual, dialogical, aesthetic, mystical or religious, iconographical, anthropological, heuristical, phenomenological, spiritual, existential, pedagogical, mysterio-logical, each desire will rise will pass will rise will intermingle with each other to form complexes which will rise pass then rise then pass then rise then pass. And there are those two attendants, so calmly holding those doors open for as long as—who knows? Nothing you do to her interrupts this, Tassiossu.

The Emergency itself. Today I was in the office again, this afternoon. Rifling through old bureaucratic papers, shuffling the history of the Emergency, each day of it and its hundred proclamations. So now, is the Emergency over? What began it, really? When? Was there an Emergency? I thought of writing a history of it, but that interests me less than writing this journal, less than categorizing my plants, the vegetation around here, flora and fauna. Animal, vegetable, mineral. This part of the work brings me closer to my wife, who loved agriculture, who wanted us to farm, even, though I called it a fantasy of hers, a dream of a better world which in fact would have been a harsher, more difficult world. She worked in our garden year round, pretending, I think, that she was farming hundreds of acres. She loved to learn about bone meal, nitrogen, manure, acidic balances and imbalances. Now it's me who gathers these plants together to form a rapport. It has happened that these plants themselves, this horticulture of my own making— let me record an example: I found a cactus which flowered in November. I found another cactus which flowered a few weeks later. I compared them. They share certain traits: they both have round, tubular stems. They are both taller than they are wide. Their flowers both last for about two weeks. Yet there are differences: on one, randomly growing spines guard it. For the other, a layer of cotton-shaped but stiff yellow fluff, very sharp. One of these cactuses has a complex root structure, i.e. four or more roots [my neoscientific definition of complex] growing out in different directions, whereas from the other, two roots grow straight down. I'm no scientist. I was no scientist. Now I have to make several choices. I can lump these two together into a family I would call Mid-winter Flowering Cacti. I could lump them with other cacti who have short blossoming seasons: two weeks or less. I could separate these two cacti into different root types. I've taken extensive notes now, made tentative organizations, constantly reorganize the whole system as I gather information.

But I began to write, then digressed from, that, a couple of times I have sat among the plants I work with, grown quiet among them, my respiration even in accord with their own, with a despair that itself has at least two roots: one, that all my organization is not only a vain attempt to give birth, for one man alone living alone in what was once an Emergency Settlement to begin an entire civilization, to culture a culture with my imagination alone, but that even the very categorizing itself is a ridiculous gesture in the midst of a silent (yet persevering), chaotic (yet functional) nature, or at least a nature of infinite (so uncategorizable) possibility and even infinite (so uncategorizable) difference. The other root of my despair is something less known to me, something unknowable, perhaps. Maybe. I am filled in those moments with a frustration—this sounds of course ridiculous itself, if not insane—that the plants themselves don't care. No, no. It's crazy, of course, but no one will read this. Write it down. You are free to write to say to think to be however insanely. That the plants will not care, that the sun will not care, that the desert will not care. The root of despair grows deeper then. There was that an old man I met when I first came, an immigrant from Europe by way of Africa, then here. He'd been a clothes designer who learned much about color and design while in Africa. He made me a few shirts as a gift, and a jacket. But also, he gardened. He showed me how much one could do here in the desert. He would be out in his tangled piece of land with his grizzled face moving around among flowers and vegetables. He had become as parched as the earth. Yet at those couple of times, when I have sat among the plants I've gathered, tagged with names (more than one named after my tailor-gardener friend: Myuel—was it Romanian, Swiss, African, I never knew), I have sunk into that despair. Then, it will not so much pass as exhaust itself. How long can despair last? It does not get answered, but it does wear out. It leaves behind more a sense of meaning than of defeat. There was a time in life when such despairs had remedies: go out to dinner, gather with friends, worry about money, resolve not to worry about money, make love, clean up your office. Read the newspapers. Work on some problem. Talk to someone. Make music. Underneath it all you would feel the desolation at your heels, but you had outraced it. The Emergency is over. I declare. The despair among the plants pulls you under not with gravity but with the absence of ground. You fall through a grey massless chamber. There must be some end some one. Some thing besides the distance from the plants themselves through which you could not reach out to touch them. You think of old words that might have rescued you, in the voices of those who spoke them, or your own voice, or the voice of your most detached voice. You might try to imagine places from memory which might absolve you of despair, though imagination is a constituent device at those moments demobilized, inaccessible. Certain images from the past drift further away into the grey mass, become part of its particulate. The massless grey of which you too are now composed becomes a pressure, so that you are the pressure even as you are being pressured. If that massless grey were water it would be water pressure, the deeper you sank the greater the pressure until at one moment there is the infusion of pressure so that everything you might be is that pressure your body becomes that pressure. Despair is no longer an impoverishment, but an action. By the time it is over you had given up on escaping it, and you didn't escape it. It exhausted itself, leaving you tired, so that you slept, perhaps without more meaning than defeat, even though you rarely slept in the afternoon. And often, often, in that sleep, joy would possess you. Joy rising from despair. Lightness displacing weight. Without cause. Causeless.

I read, I work on the horticulture—are you listening, my daughter, I'm talking to you? I work also on building, reconstructing. I'm a prince in a way. I've built myself three desks because I like to work in three different places. I have the one in the office, which I will usually use for going over papers from the Emergency, Government documents, reports, Tassiossu's researches, things like that. I've built a canopied desk in the garden. The canopy, moveable, can be removed altogether, swung over to protect me from the sun, or brought around to cover the whole thing up in case of rain. It leaks in the rain. Water, I've discovered, is as resourceful as fire, even more so. I've built a desk outside of town in the desert itself. I don't use it too often, but it's great for making notes of desert observations, animal field notes, personal reflections which I'll later incorporate into this writing. I'm going to begin an anthropological study of some of the animal behavior. To be truthful though (well, to whom, well, to myself, of course, it's still of value to be truthful with oneself) I don't work much at the desert desk. And I've built a desk on the porch of my apartment. Have I mentioned that the apartment itself is on the second floor, accessible from a stairway that runs along the side of the building, leads out onto a series of four porches, one of which I occupy? There I've built my desk. And there I do most of this writing (as now), although I don't want to get ahead of myself, because I was, I believe, in the process of describing my day, and I'm still in the middle of the afternoon. And I'm determined to finish that.

Here are the tools I've garnered from here and there to work with:—no wait, may I interrupt myself? Yes, you may, of course you may. Those couple of times when I sat among the plants with that despair I have just written about...eventually, both times, by the next day I realized that the despair, neither meaningful nor a defeat, in the meeting of the pressure from without and the pressure from within, was a fulfillment. It is very difficult now not to distort the experience, in reflection, not to say that it was even, in a way, in its own fulfillment. I will restrain myself from that because I don't believe I can substantiate it, and I may be adding it, revising the experience of it. It happened, though, both times, a fulfillment I would not have pursued it, but there it was. After the first time it happened, two days later, I sat among the plants and saw them kaleidoscopically, all greens yellows reds, all growing outward exponentially, expanding, breathing. That at times I sit among them in the heat of this sun almost as a plant myself, thoughtless, nearly, and only with the one human sensation of my combined senses with which I absorb the presence of these plants.

All right. Now. The tools I've garnered from here and there to work with: a hammer, three screwdrivers, an assortment of nails, a crosscut saw, a crowbar, four pairs of pliers, one of them needle-nose pliers, a pair of clamps, a collection of ropes and strings, eight wrenches, a pick, three axes, four shovels, 2 fan rakes, 2 fork rakes, trowels, gardening clippers (from Myuel's shed), 4 pushbrooms, 6 or 8 sweeping brooms, buckets, a collection of brackets, ratchets.

What else? I'd have to take an inventory. I think that's about it. I could never do what Grammatico and Hwang and those characters could accomplish with tools and material. Half of what I do works, half doesn't. Yet it feels good, as they say, to work. I never did it. I'm a Bureaucrat. People say it calms the mind, it gives you time to think. It's odd. I have all the time to think there might be. I have the whole possibility of all time to think. But working makes you think differently. So now I try to work everyday at something. The unnerving thing is that once you begin this handiwork sort of thing you see that it's endless, you keep coming up with things to do, and those things nag at you. Maybe that's good for you. But I will work for an hour or so most days. I have the pleasure of being the most ordinary of men during those times.

That prepares me to write. (We are getting toward the end of the day.) I'll wash up, sometimes change clothes, then begin to write. Every day. At first I thought to mark each entry in this writing with a date from an invented calendar. I discarded that idea. There should be no demarcation between one phrase or another, no distinct boundary in the thread of the writing. There is the writing. It began by happenstance it continues by inadvertence. Truly. It is not willed, despite its dailiness. Or, it has its own will. When I write I work mostly at the desk on my porch. From here I see many things: since the apartment building is on a hill, I see much of the Settlement. Many of the buildings, especially the great ones, the old stone masterpieces, their fallen columns, long stretches of foundation walls: the opera house, the regional post office, both churches, the museum, the courthouse, the library. I see some of the later, large brick structures. The factories, the mills, the concert hall. And some of the houses, some whose residents I knew. The streets. As we renamed them. The writing goes on in the stillness established by the presence of these unoccupied buildings. Odd, how I can look at them all, as now, and think of them as a Lucinda-concert. A violin. An instrument. It triggers the imagination with its host of senses. I am not writing for them, even to preserve them. If I wanted to preserve, I would write in stone. Do I write to complete a circle of language, a circuit of language from its origins in my mind to its substance on the page, a grounding pole. Its host of senses so when I consider the sense of touch I think just now of Alina of that one night in my room when she recounted the attack on her village while my hand traveled along the length of the side of her body. A grounding pole? Her body could be so young at times, a child's body, a girl's. She would say that to me sometimes, that my body seemed to her sometimes to be a boy's body to her. She told me once that she had taken me with her back into the physical loneliness of her childhood, that I was the lover of her physically lonely childhood, its sexual, sensual loneliness. I don't think any lover I knew had felt as close to my body as Alina. She was constantly drawn to it, lifting my shirt at some random moment in the day to touch me. If I would get up early in the morning to go do something, or wake up anxious, needing to walk out, leaving her in bed asleep, she would dream I had left her, then wake up worried that I had left her. I would remind her that she'd had the dream only because I had gotten out of bed before she'd had the chance to touch me in the morning.

How did she leave me so easily? It wasn't so easy. Yet, when she came in to say goodbye you knew she had been rehearsing it since the day she first walked into the office. How had she opened herself to me, even physically, so completely, knowing the outcome? Had she taken me—the night we lay in bed, the slight wind coming in the window, the night she told me about the invasion, the night I ran my hand along the curvature of her body—had she taken me with her into the invasion of her village the way she said she had taken me, physically, into the loneliness of her childhood? You don't know, Alina, that I climbed up onto the roof of my apartment house that afternoon to watch you walk off into the desert with your villagers. I saw you go for a long while. I must have watched for over half an hour. The sun was declining. I could still see you by the time I came down, off in the distance. It was better that way, that I came down while you were still there, in the landscape. I harbor no resentment for what happened with Empouche. I would have to be a more deeply dissatisfied man than I am to indulge in that. I know what you were doing. You were preparing yourself to detach yourself from me, as you were reminding me to be prepared. The only difference is that I didn't take you with me into the memory of my body; I took you only into its present. During all that time yours was the only body that existed in mine; mine was only my body of the present. It's the only way I could have done it. I write not even to preserve you, Alina. That could never be the purpose of this writing because it could preserve you only in such a perverse way that it would strangle the actual memory of you as it would suffocate the writing. Every act of writing you exists only in the moment of the writing, in the act of it. It is apart from my memory of you. Your skin, where my hand met your skin, as in that one night which keeps coming back to me, that was the axis of the present. It's not that it doesn't exist anymore. But having existed, for me, only in the present, it existed in time itself. That is something neither a part of, nor apart from, what I see as the continuum of a life. It exists neither before nor after, nor even during. There are no wings on either side of it, there are no angels no standard bearers on either side who might open it or close it.

My apartment building is in the Eastern Sector of the Settlement. When I write, I see the Settlement with the sun over it, on its way down. The desk faces northwest. The sun is visible, but not in my eyes. To the north of the Settlement is unexplored territory. Everything which happened or happens outside the Settlement—Alina's walk when she disappeared, the water works, the plants I have located in various places,—is to the south. When I watched Alina and her villagers depart, they headed out southwest. When the raiders came into the village they from the East, the direction of the Capital. More to the Southeast. So that behind me, while I write, is the landscape I know better, before me is the landscape I know not at all. This is not a metaphor or symbol for the writing process, that would be ridiculous. It is just the way the porch best allowed me to situate the desk comfortably without the sun being in my eyes. But it does mean that behind me, while I write, is a great deal of territory which I know well, where much has happened. It gives me the feeling strangely of being able to draw on that space, to rely on it, to trust it while I'm writing.

All of the pages I write I take into the apartment where I keep them in a drawer-lined storage trunk. I've filled four of those drawers so far, beginning with the earliest pages in the top drawer, moving down. I write in real ink, not with ball pens, because, how ironically I have chosen to do this! because the ink from ball point pens disappears after several years, while real ink lasts much much longer. What am I expecting? Someone to open the trunk, pull open a drawer, find a sheaf of papers, begin reading in an indelible ink the words upon words that are here? An advancing army? An army of salvation? Who? The Government? The enemy? No one who was here would return. How strange it would be for them to find me here, the Captain who still refuses to abandon his ship, which still refuses to quite go down. Perhaps I stay just because I want some thing to go down with. How odd to think of Tassiossu arriving back here, while I open drawer after drawer to show him what I've been up to. Guillemette. Everything is known, they say, at the very beginning of every relationship. So it was with Alina. So it was with Guillemette. When she walked into the office she carried her wild ingenuity with her. (I imagine now that I'm writing to the music played on the instrument of the remains of the Settlement.) I knew how she would engage me, and then I watched it all unfold. One must confront the feeling in one's life that everything is the acting out of some preordained constantly repetitious event. It's a feeling out of which the life-blood is drained. You look for some counterbalancing force, some unnamable unaccountable dynamism which can design space for you. When Guillemette dubbed me the Prince of the Emergency Settlement (oh, yes, Alina called me a prince as well, the Prince of the Physical Loneliness of her Childhood—I must have become quite princely somehow) it was the culmination of an event I had known. When I sat drinking with Guillemette a few days before she left I had the feeling that I had known all my life that I would sit with someone just like her, glad to be there, drinking. What do I mean, someone just like Guillemette? Wait, no, that's an aside. What I'm after is something else. What I'm after is to recognize that I never knew I would do this writing. It has no sense of precognition to it, hence no sense of repetition and no need for a counterbalancing sense of dynamism to make it go forward. Because what I'm writing is an account of a day, and I have come to account for the writing which I do now everyday. I will come back to Guillemette and the kind of person she is. Later. Perhaps.

That night we lay in his room, in his bed, with the window open. It was a warm night, there was a breeze which came in the window to blow over us. For much of the evening I lay there, my back turned to him, while telling him the story of the invasion of my village. Why this one evening sticks in my memory, I do not know. I know that I left my father alone that night to go to him. I remember the look in my father's face when I left. I'm sure he wanted me to stay with him that night, not to leave him alone, but I too couldn't be alone that night. All the time I lay there talking to him his hand caressed my body up / down traveling from my neck over my shoulder down the side of my torso over my hips down my thigh just to my knee to where he could reach without moving then back up the same way again over and over. My voice going directly from my body into the fingers of his hand. Still, I felt so badly for Papa. Having left him. Why did I tell him that whole story that particular night? Why did I lie about certain things? When I lied I felt protected. I went to him for protection that night, and then in the midst of it I had to protect myself from him. Sometimes, not all the time. We were equally vulnerable together. It was temporary, transient, fugitive. He felt settled there. I knew we were all on the run still. He wanted to plant himself and all of us there in the desert. He still believed, that's why. After the invasion of our village, there was nothing left for me to believe

I told him stories, he told me stories. He told me about his life before the Emergency Settlement, he told me about his family, his daughter, his parents, his sister, his friends, his work. He told me about life in the Emergency Settlement before we arrived. So many more came after us, filing in, columns and groups and cadres of refugees. Imagine a whole city of refugees, not one native. Where had all the natives gone? We looked together for records, and although we found papers relating to the life of the Settlement long before it became the Emergency Settlement in the Western Quadrant and in all of that we found nothing about the fate of the original inhabitants, the ones who built the buildings, the ones who laid the pipes underground, the ones who had read in the library, gone to the concert hall, wandered the streets, or prowled them. I did that. I prowled the streets often. I went out walking in the night, the nights we spent together, after he would fall asleep. Whenever I would come back, get back into bed, he would say—I thought he was dead asleep—he would ask me, Where have you been? I would answer him, using that word: Prowling the streets, I would say. He wouldn't say anything, he would hold me, then he would lie awake for some time while I slept. His turn to prowl. The time I came to him after it began with Empouche—something which didn't last long—I arrived in the late afternoon. He suspected I had already been with Empouche that day, which I hadn't. Why did I start with Empouche? I don't know. Something propelled me with an urgency I could not understand. It wasn't like me. I've changed so much because of the Emergency. I will never remember who I was. That's what I told Guillemette when we talked once. And I asked her: do you remember who you were? She said that she hadn't changed so much, that despite everything she was still Guillemette. Perhaps because she had never felt terribly stable or secure in her knowledge of who she was it was easier for her to adapt herself to the Emergency, to go on being who she was, enigmatic as it was. To organize the festivals, to hold workshops with her group, Il Gruppo delle Idee Fabbricate she called them, among other things. She told me once that she had plans to do a festival in which she used the whole desert around us as the sea, that it would become the sea. Everyone from the Settlement would come out to the desert, to a spot she and Hwang had found on a long walk, where they would be the audience. They would be so convinced, she said, that they were at sea, they would wonder how to get back to the Settlement after it was all over. She took me out there once to have a look at it. The way she talked, she had me almost convinced we were at sea. She swept her hand out over the landscape of small plants, rocks, lizards, hillocks of desert ground, she made it, with her descriptions, shimmer like a sea, roll like a sea, contain the kind of solitude we feel the sea engenders in us, undulate with the kind of life force we always imagine the sea to contain. Guillemette's worlds were more real than the world in which we lived, the one in which I lived. Her festivals created worlds—I don't mean they were so real they were like my real world, I mean that literally they were more real than my world. More actual. More fundamentally existent. They were not trying to portray our world, they were another, more substantive, more believable reality than our own. I told this once to Alina, who had not seen the original festival, the one with the monstrous spider, but it was impossible to explain to her. I told her to go out with the Gruppo one day to watch them in the desert working on their sea piece. She came back understanding what I had tried to explain to her. That's what my writing seems to me now, as I write this. An explanation which cannot explain. It is not meant to. That is not its purpose. It has no purpose. It exists. How can it have a purpose? How can it not? It takes place each day at about the same time. It occurs without my willing it. What I have seen I have no name for, it is not the intention of this writing to name it.

Guillemette was the only one here who had not suffered some kind of unremembering in the face of the Emergency. I used to imagine that she must have come from very tough circumstances, so that for her the Emergency was just one more of them. But in fact, I found out, she came from very cozy circumstances, wealthy parents, good schools, success in her work. That's why I wanted to talk about her, to write her, to approach the enigma of her in the writing, so that the enigma might turn, showing me the edges of itself. She confessed to me that she had little sense of herself as a person, that asked to identify herself, she couldn't do very well, that asked to talk about her aspirations, she couldn't name them, that she only knew the same confusion before the Emergency, during the Emergency, during her life in the Emergency Settlement. That she knew how to work in her kind of theater. Was it, I asked her once, over a beer in the drain of the heat toward the end of the day, that her theater was a world so much more real than our own that she could identify herself only there, only in her theater, but it was an identity which had no words in our own language to describe it? She laughed. It was a complicated question, she said, too complicated perhaps for herself. When I asked it, she said, she had a vision. She saw a large, six or seven foot panel. She saw it from the side, so that each face of the panel looked in a different direction, one to the left of her, one to the right of her. Each panel was a mirror, reflecting sunlight. She couldn't answer my question, but the panels might well become, she said, a construction at the center of another festival piece. A vivid image, she said, a productive possibility. She thanked me for asking the question which, she said, she couldn't remember, and she apologized for not answering it. If, she said, I could re-phrase the question, she would do her best. I drank my beer. She snacked on that famous treat of the Emergency Settlement: small squares of garlic toast and beer. We invented nearly everything here. Can I believe what we actually did? What questions could I possibly pose of it?

At one point I had decided to end each writing with a

phrase taken from that day's work. That too is not a good idea. It's like a date, or a heading. The writing should be a continuum, a wave, not a particle. Can I tell where a day's work ended? Is there a rhythm to it? I'm beginning to ask questions not about the writing, but about the written. Is that another stage? A taxonomy of writing, as of cacti. An anthropology of the artifact? Are there stages? I imagine there are. Could I go back over the scriptures (now that's a funny word for it, given its history, but one that came to mind. No comparison intended—I mean the script-ed, as in a great line of script-ing dating back to the hand in the cave—I'm a Bureaucrat, I need a greater vocabulary) to discover a series of stages? There is a certain progress to writing out the pattern of a day, but it's only the progress of a day itself. I won't dwell on the written work, on its nature. I'll write it. I can exercise all my desire to examine, categorize, explain on the work of nature. It's a more reasonable object to focus on.

I have written at each of my three desks. I've taken paper out to the desk in the desert on occasion—a few times. The first time because I couldn't write. I looked for a change of something. Place was what I could change. I carried the materials for the desk out to the desert, then built it there, in situ. It belongs to the place. Near the canyon. Just east of there. That first day, after I'd finished building, I sat down to work. It was getting late, but as I'd written every day, it was important to get something down. I sat for a while first, looked at the paper, the ink pen, my hands. I waited as every thought passed out of my mind. What I had to write had nothing to do with thought. I had always thought (well, to use the word again, what can I do? I am not trapped in words, but the writing is circumscribed by them—in circumscriptions which layer transparently one over another) that thought itself was what I wrote. That was a mis-vision. My right hand holding the pen, my hands, still as they were, an animate phenomenology. I turned them over to look at the palms. I flexed the fingers. Whose are these? Fantastical. Desert lizards, about to dart around the just-made desk in ways which I could follow with my eyes, now also two other desert lizards. At the outermost, extreme boundary of the mind/body conundrum, I saw my body as I might see a lizard, held stock still in my gaze. A rock. The piece of paper. The pen. It wasn't that my body was objectified, merely. It lived. Veins, scars, little sores. I examined my fingernails because they almost perceptively grow. I lifted my hands. They floated in that dry air. Having no notion of what mind is, it's better to say a consciousness/body conundrum, as it was clear to me just then that the two, consciousness and body, cohabiting, each perhaps within the other, would never quite answer each other except nearly at the slippage of some uninimitable near-moment. This gulf of truancy between them preposterous extreme incongruous farcical extravagant. It was a space beyond...what? I wanted to write: beyond sorrow, and so I will write that, right or wrong, beyond sorrow.

Aware, in this particular state of my body, of the hairs growing on my hands, the tingling sensation in my legs signaling a relaxation, the movement of my eyes across the landscape, aware of the mechanism of vision as light passing through along nerves into the brain, and having let all thought go by, I took the pen to write one word. The first word I wrote would be an insurmountable commitment of scription made in the open breach by the body to the consciousness. Or the other way around. That word no less a body than my own. Blue ink. This blue Italian ink pen Grammatico had given me. The manufacturer's identifying commercial words inscribed on the nub too small to read. Made by someone. Whatever word. I could have written Emergency. War. Horror. Emptiness. As well as Grammatico, desert, hand, Alina, love.

I did begin writing again. The change of place had worked as a device. Writing there, at that desk in the desert, it is most clear that there is nothing to say: the word will not span the gap which will never be empty of the word. The saying of that of which there is nothing to say will multiply, branch off, twist, turn, recombinate, regenerate, continue, even as it never leaves the locus of its imaginary origin, even as, in all its wanderings it contains that locus. When I might exhaust the resources of my language, it will perform an unwilled metamorphosis of its own to become a new language.

Now, just now, as I'm writing, see it, yes, not only am I writing to no one, but also there is nothing to say. Nothing to say, I write. And I write it again, nothing to write.

Is this my freedom or the end of a freedom. To go on writing. I have arrived now, just now—not then, when I came here, but just now at this very moment I have arrived at the Emergency Settlement. Although I am not at the desk in the desert just now, but at the desk on the porch from where I can see the Emergency Settlement, as I look around, just now, I write: that's nonsense, what I see with my eyes, those public buildings, those houses, these streets, that City Abandoned, my own house, my office, that's the Emergency Settlement, there it is before your eyes. Look at it. Real as day. Substantial as what? But it's not nonsense, is it? But it is, isn't it? The Emergency Settlement, where I arrive now is where there is nothing to say to be said. There is no one to read this because there is nothing to be said. Because what has to be said cannot be heard. Quiet your hand. Look at it: that very substance of that very Settlement is the very fact of this crisis. Isn't it? There it is: all being said. The less I write the more it is said. The more I write the more it is said.

I'm frantic now, even writing frantically, I can see, I mean my handwriting, trying to salvage something. Haven't yet I learned yet to lose things? There is no difference between what I see and what I write, I mean as objects, that both exist simultaneously coming into being going out of being coming into being going out of being. I can say that someone will find this writing, that it will be read, I can insist to myself, even against the most foundational premise I have agreed to accept: that it is written to no one. Even as I address one person after another, even unknown persons, readers. I can assure myself: don't worry: you won't lose the writing. No matter what it comes to you'll do it every day. I can rescue it from the truths of itself because as good fortune has it I have some mechanism within me where truth is irrelevant.

Was that awareness, that first time there at the desk in the desert the result of a loneliness of the body? Because I was no longer touched or touching other bodies? A disconnection? Perhaps. (Go on.) Have those books I discovered among Tassiossu's things—books on religious or mystical sexuality— led me to think more about the body? The body of the Madonna, say, (going on) or the body of the Infant Child in the poster in my office. Of course, Alina's body. My wife's body. Alive. Please. I can only think of it as alive. I refuse other visions of it. I have the strength of refusal. Don't I? Each time I go to the desert to write I have hallucinations from which I always manage to return. Or I have different experiences of my own presence. Or a loss of touch with ordinary language, so that for a time I will be incapable of writing. These are a little frightening in their way, yes, but pleasurable also, voyages. Unknowns. I get more and more used to them. They haven't unfastened me from whatever moorings hold me now. They work to my good, I am refreshed in them. In useful madnesses. I work. I get connected to the work, abandoned in the work (yes, going on), in the writing. When it's over for the day I'll get up to return, carrying the day's sheets of paper with me. By the time I get back to the edge of the Settlement, I'm thinking again about the life here, about some festival we held, some dinner, something I did as Governor of the Settlement, about my wife, even about the next day. Life, even the invented life or the contrived life or the memoriac life has a hold of me again. I come home, I put the papers away in the cabinet, I get on with the evening. I've done my work. I've achieved enough.

freedom. enough.

So: I have a domestic desk, the one on the porch, the desk of civilization; then I have the desert desk, what should I call that, the desk of the wilderness? then I have the desk in the garden, and what would that be, the desk of cultivation?

After writing each day I'll have a drink. I'll take it with me somewhere, on to the roof of my apartment, downtown into some ruin, out to the edge of the Settlement, just into the desert, or walk a ways into the open. The other day I took my evening drink down to where I had seen the young couple on the walk my first day here, in the Settlement. The ruins of the Post Office building, over three hundred years old. I could wonder what happened to that young couple, where they are now, but that would be a sentimental thing to do. Already, that first day, I imagined they represented something, a contrast, a choice, even an inevitability. They were lovers, there were the ruins. Now it seems there is nothing represented, no contrast, no choice, not even fate perhaps, but just the fact: two lovers, ruins of the Post Office. If all time exists at once, as Alina liked to say it did, then those lovers and those ruins were (or are, or some other word I do not know) absolved of contrast, absolute in a conditional sense. In a mundane way, those lovers were there the day I walked past the ruins with the President. With his entourage, I should say. I might have killed him myself if I'd been left alone with him. On that day those lovers were there, talking, drinking coffee, in much the same way that I heard the gunshot in the Presidential office as I left, yet I heard it only months later, the sound having traveled at a much,

much slower speed than the scientists report. I confessed both to Tassiossu and to Alina that I heard it, and then later to Abanno, and all three of them believed I had actually heard it. Believed the President had actually shot that Bureaucrat—whom I had known—in the outer office, that day. Believed, Tassiossu and Alina and Abanno believed that it had indeed taken two months for that sound to reach my ears. In the same way those two lovers were there the day I walked by that ruin with the President.

We would have all killed him. Empouche and Guillemette and Hwang urged me to it. I told them to lay a plot if they could. Go ahead, I said, do it. It won't do any good, I said, but do it if you can be sure you will all three of you get away with it. Do it for me, I told them. I know that the President came to make sure I wasn't getting out of line. I fantasized the assassination would lead to an uprising which would begin in the Settlement, spread to the Capital, put an end to the Emergency, to the wars, establish peace. We'd be revered. We'd have done something other than learn to survive. I knew it was idle. It reminded me of the fantasies that filled me as a child. No plot could succeed against the protection with which the President surrounded himself, even on our turf. That's the argument Empouche pressed, that he would be on our turf. I set them up as the Assassination Council: Guillemette and Hwang were to hatch plots to kill the President, Empouche was to prove how they would fail. They worked like mad over those three days, but Guillemette and Hwang couldn't outsmart Empouche. When the President arrived in town with a contingent of three hundred soldiers the Council scrapped everything. They still wanted to go after it, but I convinced them they might only kill the President, be surely killed themselves, and leave the Settlement impoverished of their lives, which we needed. Am I will I always be such the practical Bureaucrat? Why didn't I let them go ahead with it? Kill him. At least get revenge before dying, one moment's brute satisfaction. We should have gone ahead with it. I would have been killed as well. Of course. Executed in public, perhaps right there, in front of the ruins of the Post Office, it would have been a good place. Who could give a damn? Then what, fifty or a hundred or five hundred residents in the Settlement? People I was trying to protect. Ah, you go on. You reason to yourself. Those were your reasons. Were you right? Is there a difference? The President is dead. Or so I had heard. After the rule of thumb became to believe only what I hadn't heard. Figure that out, that will keep you busy. Read it like the *Page* of Meleq's novel.

What if I resumed my duties as Director of the Emergency Settlement. Just a thought. As though the Settlement were as it had been. What if someone arrived, found me administering a Settlement which no longer exists? Acting out all the roles of Administrator. They would think me mad, but it would be a preservation of sanity to do so, to assume a phantom role, allow myself to hear the voices of those who are gone—other than in the dim way I do hear them now—go about filling out papers, making plans, holding meetings. They would think they had found a madman, but they would not. If only I could allow myself to cross that line, and in the end it is not such a distant line, is it? Looking back through these pages I found: "...all pleasure partakes of madness, pantomime, silliness, transgression, and the validation of the seemingly false which is actually not the true false." Maybe someday I will give myself that allowance, I will slip into it, I will not question it. It would keep me from the gloom I keep at bay by writing. I will do it. For myself. No. No one will come, no one will find you like that. As no one will read this manuscript. No one will discover you acting your role. But the role will be so close to what I was, what I am. What am I? I am afraid to slip into that because it will go on without end and then I will be lost? Lost from what? Into what? From isolation into solitude, living in a world no one else concurs with? Only I concur with the world I live in now, only I. What I? Would I quit writing? Quite likely I would. I would have to. Why? Because writing would reveal the truth to me. What truth? The truth that would be revealed to me through writing. That one. What is more valuable to you: to write in your notebooks, or to resume your duties as Governor of the Emergency Settlement? From now on that choice will always be yours, and maybe it is for the sake of the choice itself, to maintain the choice, that you consider it.

It is something like this. Dear Tassiossu, I have been thinking lately, really a great deal, about your work on the Madonna. I have come up with some things I would like to talk to you about. First, we have very little iconography of the Virgin's death. Isn't that strange? We have the Annunciation a hundred times, we have a hundred times that hundred images of the Madonna with the Christ Child, the flight (probably mythical, you had said) into Egypt, images with the crucified Christ, but none of her death. Then, going through your papers recently, I found one. A painting. Some notes. You were aware of it, you are aware of it, but you never mentioned it. In your notes you talk about how rare it is in the iconography. You give it its name: Transgressus Mariae. You talk about the one painting you do have a photograph of. In your notes you speculate that Christian culture can live with imagery of the Madonna in nearly every circumstance, every position, every emotion. But Christian culture cannot live with the *absence* of the Madonna. You question the Bible, to discover its mention in the Bible, but you hadn't finished that part of your work. You were searching Apocrypha. Let's talk about this, Tassiossu. What culture could live without its concomitant image? With the absence of its parallel image? But I like this image, Tassiossu, this image of her absence. Her death not in an iconographic or historical or religious sense, but in the mythical sense which I realize I share, have shared unconsciously until I saw this one picture you had, read your notes.

The Transgressus Mariae is not a trip to heaven, like Christ's; not a trip to hell, like Lucifer's. It is a fact of absence. (How can one have a *fact* of *absence?*) This is something we need to talk about, you and I. We need to walk around the streets here like we used to do, talking. I think we would agree on this, we would see how important it is that this is an apocryphal image, a marginalia nearly erased by the canonical powers. It's the most radical discovery you made, yet you never talked to me about it. Were you holding it back? Did you, yourself, not want to think about it? A funny thing, Tassiossu, but after all we talked about these images, after my fascination with your fascination, I look out at the Settlement, the desert, my house, my office to see the world without the filter of that Madonna image. It seems to me a world cleared of a film. Even inwardly, I look at memory, even the memory of my discussions with you. They seem cleared of a film. The absence of the Madonna is the one topic you didn't broach. You would talk about her mundanity, her humanness, her sexuality, innocence, courage, tenderness, motherliness, ignorance, divinity, but not her absence. Now I discover it. Now.

And here's the other thing. Dear Tassiossu. The idea of the absence of the Madonna leads me to another important aspect of the Madonna as you presented her to me: the most significant fact in all those images is their difference. The same figure represented differently in different ages by different people. In the same age by different people. Differently over time by the same artist. Her absence inherent in all her manifestations. In each of her manifestations.

How is it, Tassiossu, that the absence of the Madonna magnifies the presence of other things, such as you? My image of you? I could say that her absence is your absence and that magnifies the presence of you, but it is only partly true. The other is wholly true: her absence simply magnifies the presence of other things. Either she is not included in other things, or her absence is included in them. Either way. Things

SETTLEMENT

are clarified for me. How is it? How is it I do not fall into some satisfying madness of becoming the Governor of a non-existent Emergency Settlement? For it would be madness, and if they found me like that they would be right: I would be mad, but I cannot tell you, Tassiossu, what madness is. No, let me make it better: I cannot tell you what not-madness is.

I am trying to tell you, Tassiossu, about the progress of my day. After writing, I will go out with a drink...that's where I got stuck yesterday, wasn't it? I was talking about going out for a drink and I began to talk of other things. Those two young lovers. How large was their love yet how much had it learned to contain of things which they never imagined love would lead them to? Lying in bed with Alina, stroking her body, the wind coming through the window that night. I wonder about Tassiossu and his Madonna. The Christians call it Original Sin but that's hubris there is no origin for it. There has been no crime. But of course...I should have killed the President. I myself. Only me. They would have killed me and been satisfied, left all the others alone. The concert I arranged a concert for that evening...Lucinda would play for the President. I am so stupid. I actually believed it would teach him something. So much had I come to believe in silence. Her silence. How is it that a man such as myself, so innocent, a criminal so innocent of the world, has managed to survive? Perhaps I am not so naïve. Knowing the limits of my weaponry, I use what I have. If I throw darts at bombs at least I am not sitting still. Although that is an idea, too. To sit still. To watch the bomb fall.

That night, after the President cancelled the concert, Alina,

164

Lucinda and I had dinner in a beautiful desolation. From cans, jars, boxes, Lucinda made a dinner of capers, anchovies, oils, pastas. Sharp, dark flavors. We wanted then to go on living in the midst of our unspoken understanding that the end of our lives or the end of our lives together must be very close now. I had one of the bottles of French wine I had originally brought with me to the Settlement. There are still three of them left. I've opened one more bottle on my own, since being on my own. Now there are three left of the original twelve. That was the night Alina said: I envy you, Lucinda, your talent.

But Lucinda answered: Yes. I too, envy me my talent, she said. The irony slipped right past my ordinary reasoning into a realm of irony of self-knowledge. I laughed immediately, instinctively, while it shocked Alina, who didn't begin to laugh for half a minute. Then we all three laughed together. Our laughter became contagious. It contained all our anxiety. We were just drunk enough from the wine. It was a communion of laughter. The whole night went on like that while in the offices Abanno held meetings with various ministers who had accompanied the President, and, for about 15 minutes, Abanno told me the next day, he met with the President himself. Abanno, reporting how he came to like the man in that short time. How he came to believe in the President's good purpose, thought that the man had noble, worthy ideals. Felt his intentions as authentic, even ardent, Abanno said. Even saw, he said, a softness in the President, a sadness. I argued with Abanno. I never told him about the role I am sure the President had in the deaths of my wife and my daughter.

I cautioned him. I called him naïve, unworldly, innocent. I made him tell me what the President had said about me, how the President praised me, called me a most able Governor, an inspiriting leader. Oh, yes, the President told Abanno, your Governor may have some shortcomings, all men have shortcomings, but overall look at what he has accomplished: the incipient waterworks, the community activities, the levels of production from some of the industries, the textile works, the brick factory. It's all so obvious! I yelled at Abanno. The President came here because we are useless now. He's making a military reconnaissance trip, evaluating strategic options. He praised me to you, Abanno, then allowed for my shortcomings! He was baiting you. He was fishing for disloyalties. No doubt you inadvertently gave him some, something. We should have killed him, I burst into rage.

I asked Abanno to tell me: what did you see in the President, what were his good purposes, his noble, worthy ideals? His authentic intentions? Tell me, I said, about the softness in him, the sadness that you saw. Abanno said that after this meeting he believed that the President detested the Emergency, the wars, that he had the peoples' interests at heart, that he talked about the possibilities of brotherhood, of a spreading natural affection for all mankind which will come when civil life returns. The odd thing is that as Abanno spoke, I believed not the President, but Abanno. Hwang. I'm sorry. Can you see what I was doing, what I tried to balance? What's the point of my life, of the writing of these journals in the face of what happened to you, Hwang? But that's exactly it. What could be the point of my life if I did not write these journals, in the face of what happened to you, Hwang? Writings without which the cataclysm of the end of your life would engulf everything consciousness had by which it might live. The writing which is not a protest, not a witness, not a communication, not a record, neither a declaration of faith nor a grief-song at the loss of faith. I wish it were all of those. Even one of them. I accept that it is none of them. It is something much more.

Abanno. You saw what happened to Hwang. How we sat all afternoon the day after your visit with the President. That was the first night that I slept out, wasn't it? on the rooftop where Grammatico had built a bed for us. Although I slept alone that night, without Alina. I had gone to work after you left, Abanno, for I was the Administrator, a Bureaucrat, one who served the people below him, not one who pleased the people above him. My famous motto. There was much to do.

I am the Genius of Bureaucracy. In the breached space of the real I can discover the idea of the real. In the uncovered actuality of the unreal I name the fabric of space. I am capable of such magic .

Perhaps I would come to the end of my telling of a day in my life now only to just begin again, with the next morning. No, that would be too funny. I would then have to write constantly, every minute. The only thing I would write about would be the act of writing at the moment of writing. (The only thing I would write would be the act of writing at the moment of writing.) But I will try to finish telling you (who? my daughter? who? my friend Tassiossu? who the book itself?) about my day, a task I can't hardly seem to get done what with interruptions coming faster. So...the progress of my day...I will take a drink, go somewhere with it. Often I will imagine some conversation I might have with someone, with one of you, over this drink. I will remember the old life often then, some art show we had gone to before the Emergency began, some evening we spent with friends, something we did together. Here, at the still light end of the day, I can relax. I can think about dinner, look to the pleasure I take in cooking. Bureaucrat that I am, I will try to manage with what I've got for dinner, making the most of it. I will feel sadness sometimes at this hour, a melancholy will infect me, a welcome melancholy from which I know I will emerge, ready enough to be in the night.

Why this impulse to describe a typical day? I will have encompassed something. Passed on something concrete. Some graspable tale for someone to read. At night I will do this and such. After dinner, I will light a candle, if I feel there is something to do worth using up one candle. If I want to read something of Tassiossu's notes, a novel Meleq left behind, which in fact I never do tire of reading with immense pleasure, if I want to go over my own writings, if I want to make notes on my plant biology, my animal studies, my bird watchings, if I want to go over inventories, which, for some odd reason, I find myself keeping like the Bureaucrat I am. Knowing how much of something—how many candles, for example—I have left will make some difference in my life. I skipped writing about dinner, didn't I? Yes. I did. Although I somewhere in these writings I talked about it. Nonetheless, it's important to keep that part of this writing—the telling of the day—in order.

I used to cook a lot for other people, so that now cooking reminds me of those other times. It helps to keep me human, rekindles the presence of social life in the absence of it. Alina, who was a good cook, preferred nonetheless that I cooked because it made her feel taken care of. I liked taking care of her. Easy enough now to fall into the desuetude of not cooking for myself, bad enough to fall into it so that I must cook dinner each night. Gather the elements: cans, boxes, water, fresh elements from around me, cactus leaves, for example, yucca. Some things I've found to eat I don't know the names of at all. Although in my organizational notes I have assigned names to all these things. I will often think of others when cooking, others for whom I've cooked: my wife, my daughter, Abanno, Tassiossu, Alina, of course, her parents on occasion.

I will lay a table each night for dinner. Mostly, I eat quietly. I will try not to eat too quickly, a temptation when you are alone. To eat alone. Sometimes, I will talk aloud to myself, in conversation. I will think things over. Now, as I write it, I seem a comic figure there, alone, eating, talking, alone, talking to so many. A mimic. A mime. All comic is sentimental, yes? More sentimental than the tragic, yes? Now I'm becoming a literary critic. Eventually I will germinate a whole culture here. Literary criticism. A culture based on things I know nothing about. What I do know about—what is Bureaucracy, the Bureaucrat? One who organizes living among the living. Or is the tragic more sentimental, actually? Ah, here I go. A debate with myself that propels me into the future, which will go on and on. What do I know of the tragic? Literally? Hamlet. Oh, Oedipus, of course. I am not out to discover if the tragic or the comic is the more sentimental form in literature. I'm asking myself: is the tragic or the comic impulse in life the more sentimental. I look to literature to answer that.

In the comic we laugh until we cry; no, we laugh to uncover a crying which we cannot cry, which we do not cry. In the tragic we cry....no, we are frightened...until....we laugh again? With a laughter we cannot laugh, do not laugh? Whose true laughter we approach? Whose true laughter we have laughed, a few times in our lives? But by sentimental I mean, which—the tragic or the comic—more contains an idea of life which does not really exist in life. Authentic life. Well, there's a sentimental idea, no? So both, comic and tragic, both contain an idea which does not exist in life, in external life, meaning that both are equally sentimental. But that is the whole idea. Only through the sentimentality of the tragic and that sentimentality of the comic do we know that neither the tragic nor the comic standing alone truly exists in life.

So there I am. At my dinner table. A comic figure, or at least I was for a moment, thinking about it, a comic figure to myself. Seeing myself with some oversize shoes, some outsized suit, sitting at my mock dinner party. But Now, here, I am sobered from such comedy. Which is perhaps the most comical position: this sobriety. I wish, right now, to break the surface of this silence. Which I have filled in with the sounds of the desert, the sounds of the day or night, the sounds of the

Emergency Settlement as its body shifts and changes, mutates, moves. Always there will be some sound for us to fill in with.

I look back over what I wrote yesterday (I wasn't supposed to say that; I was to have a seamless document without breaks in the writing from one day to the next; so I have broken my own rule; what is the purpose of a rule but to delineate your work out of the chaos from which it originates and which is the one thing you might say and cannot say because you must, in order to work, delineate. What does it mean then to break your own rule? It means to write the idea of rule itself, which is to approach a writing of the chaos. It means to acknowledge the artifice of your craft, which is a way to signal its desire for artlessness.) All right, then, as I look back over what I wrote yesterday in my mood as literary theorist, I am moved to think of other aspects of my work, my scription, my commitment, my daily return to this deviated point in the cycle. With no one to write to and with nothing to say, it becomes possible to evolve a form for the work, not some unconscious half-formed rules intuitively achieved (nothing wrong with those), but to think through some problems.

Come back to the description of the day. After dinner I will feel sleepy, usually. But I won't sleep. I protect my good sleep by going to bed late enough each night and getting up early enough each morning that I am tired again by the next night, and can sleep. The horror of sleeplessness, of falling into a pattern of it. Real fatigue could destroy me now. To prevent myself from falling asleep right after dinner, I will clean up, then walk in the night air. A normal thing to do, to walk through the streets as though closing down a day in which something has been lived. Walking, as though other people were inside their homes.

I walk along as though others were going to sleep. As though life here were normal. At this time of night, during these walks, I have the most freedom of thought. Thoughts now have no consequence, I take them lightly. Last night, for example, I was walking through the old neighborhood where Abanno lived. I felt that I better not disturb him, that it was too late. And I laughed. I was thinking then about all the conversations I had with him about the native plants, in those days when we were still calculating the possibility of a self-sufficiency for the Settlement. The plans we were hatching. Water works; native agricultural development. We were mad. We were clever. We were ourselves, surviving, planning survival. Your tales of how you would be out on some wilderness adventure, starving, alone, finally to discover some new source of food: some small animal overlooked, some leaf, some bark. I loved to hear you tell them, tell how you would then figure out how to gather that food, store it until you reached other sources again.

By the end of my walk I am tired. I will go home, my body as light as my head often is at that hour, and, getting into bed, sleep soundly until dawn.

I have done it, then. I have finished, within my book, my journal the telling of the cycle of one day. Funny. Yesterday I wrote about Abanno, now today I discover a new source of food. It's the fleshy-leaves of a low growing plant. I'd seen it before but hadn't noticed the leaves. I sautéed them with just a bit of oil, just a bit of garlic paste. If only I could grow garlic in the garden. If I could find a clove of it in someone's house, somewhere. How funny that I was just writing about Abanno's wilderness discoveries. I'll call this plant Abanno, I'll call the leaves Abanno leaves. I'll have some tonight again. Just a bit bitter. It gives you a queer feeling. You would like to believe even that Abanno himself had something to do with it, his skill, his experience out trekking in wildernesses of every kind. If you came back, Abanno, I would make you Abanno leaves, especially if you brought just one lemon with you to squeeze on them.

Do you remember that time Abanno and you and Alina and Grammatico played cards half the night, more than half. (I love how I ask myself that question: Do you remember...? As a prelude, an excuse for telling a story. All right. I won't tell the story now. The story of the night you (you!) and Alina and Abanno and Grammatico played cards half the night, more than half the night. What's that worth, that story? To recall it? Nothing. Find a better amusement. Write again about the night Alina spent telling you about the invasion of her village. Write about the other performance that the Gruppo delle Macchine _____ gave. You (you!) are petulant with your work tonight, aren't you? Dissatisfied? Find a way out of it, then. A way to write yourself out of it. How? By writing what? By talking about how you remember all this that has happened all the while with the belief buried in the irrationality of your primitive belief that none of it has really happened and that if you write it enough you will one day look up to find that everything has returned. Because you know that you do not have the courage to have lived all this that you write. Because you wonder who it was who did live it? Who is it who does live it? Who is it, not certainly the you of your constant address to yourself. You, who, all the time you cook your meals deny that you are here alone, cooking a meal of rations which will you someday will exhaust. Leaving you to eat of the Abanno's Leaves. You who, recalling certain events, going over and over them, recreating them, laugh at how you are immersed in a project whose purpose is invisible but whose success you insist on. Relish. Because invisibility of purpose itself is what must be recalled every day. Now. Go on, crack open the silence of your petulant mood so the words will flow out of you. Are you angry with them, themselves? The words? Don't be. Come on. They are not at fault for anything. Go on. Finish your book. Remember how (there you go again, remember how!) as an infant the words came to you. Came out of you. I do remember that and here they are, still coming out of me, still, even writing how I am petulant this evening, how I don't want to write, how I resent the words themselves, each word. How I go on writing, in a kind of self-deceiving way, hoping to deceive myself enough, with words, at words, with the voice of words, to go on, with the words. Admit it, with the joy of them. The pleasure. Oh, your petulance. Admit it. Why hold back? You want to fill pages and pages with them. Do you think the cave-man with his cave-painting of his hand wanted to fill the cave with hand paintings? Spitted hand paintings. Do you think he sat there, after he'd first done it, laughing. Then again, after he'd done it a hundred times, laughing. We took it so solemnly when we saw it. Maybe it was a great joke to him. An irrational joke. Something he laughed at because it relieved him into laughter with something he didn't understand. Understand? A modern concept. From the cave hand spit painting to Tassiossu's Madonna's. Did the cave-man, right up there, not very far from here, geographically, and truly not very far from here temporally, did he come back to his hand-art to contemplate it? Did it ever become serious for him, an object of beauty? awe? tragedy? comedy? ecstasy? fate? Did he talk to himself the way I talk to myself, giving all these names: myself, you, yourself, do you remember, etc. Did he say to himself: Look what you've done. Who was that whole tribe he must have lived with, two miles from here? Who was he? Nobody? Somebody? Everybody? Everything? Hand Spit No One In Particular? Making of the extant world of hand earth pigment cave wall some thing.

MARTIN NAKELL : *The Myth of Creation* (Parentheses Writing Series), a chapbook of fiction, *Ramon*, and the novels *The Library of Thomas Rivka* (Sun & Moon Press) and *Two Fields That Face & Mirror Each Other* (2001, Sun & Moon Press). Winner of the Gertrude Stein Award in Poetry for 1996-1999 and an NEA Interarts Grant, he was also a finalist for the America' s Award in Fiction, 1997 (for *The Library of Thomas Rivka*), a finalist in the New American Poetry Series for 1999.

Nakell has published poetry and fiction extensively in journals, including recent publications of poetry in Proliferations (San Francisco), Ribot (Los Angeles), ReMap (Boston and Los Angeles), and fiction in Literal Latte (New York), Hanging Loose (New York), Hyper Age (San Francisco), Subvoicity (London). Three chapters from Two Fields That Face and Mirror Each Other have been published in literary journals, including Washington Review and Onyx.

He has held fellowships from the Fine Arts Work Center, Provincetown (poetry), from the Blue Mountain Center (fiction and screenwriting), from Writers and Books (poetry and fiction), from the State University of New York at Albany; he has received grants from the National Endowment for the Arts, from Chapman University, from the University of California. He was a panelist for the America Awards in fiction for 1998, a panelist for the Los Angeles Arts Commission in 1999, and serves on the panel of the "100 Most Important Books of the Twentieth Century" for The Encyclopedia of Twentieth Century Literature of The Contemporary Arts Educational Project, Inc. Recently, Visual Poetics, Inc., a Los Angeles film company, optioned three of his short stories (*Ramon; Thomas; Monsieur B., The Irish Poet*), for a film entitled *A Heisenberg Trilogy*.

Martin Nakell earned a Doctorate of Arts from the State University of New York at Albany, and is Professor of Literature at Chapman University, and Visiting Professor in Creative Writing at the University of California at San Diego.

SPUYTEN DUYVIL
Meeting Eyes Bindery
Triton